Fragments

....

Lia Chris

Contents

CHAPTER ONE

In a small town, just a few miles off the main city of Edmonton, a group of teenage boys were throwing hoops at the central court. The place was battered and run down. The clay ground was corroded, and the paint that set the lines was fading off. Despite all that, there was a smile on everyone's face as they passed a worn-out basketball amongst themselves in sweat-drenched tee-shirts and pants.

"What are you looking at? Pay attention, man," One of the boys, Karl, said to Quinn before tossing the ball at his friend. It hit Quinn in the back, making the boy turn around in shock as the ball bounced off his back and on the floor for a while before sitting still. The other boys laughed. Quinn seemed to have snapped out of his daze. He bit down on his bottom lip, pushing his dark hair away from his face before picking up the ball and throwing it back to Karl.

"Shut up, I was thinking," Quinn said as Karl caught the ball with a grin on his face. The boys weren't tall or anything. Most of them stood between 5'7 to 5'10, but there wasn't much to do in such a small neighborhood aside from playing sports, smoking blunts, and drinking alcohol.

"Of course, you were," Karl said, sarcasm lacing every word. He passed the ball to Hozier, the tallest lad in the group who then made to throw a basket. The game picked up again, and soon the little quibble between Karl and Quinn was forgotten and drowned out with the background noise of yelling boys, the bouncing ball, and stampeding feet.

From time to time Quinn would look towards the gates again, catching the figure of the boy that was sitting at the stairs. He had been there for hours, and Quinn wondered why he didn't just come up and join them.

Why does he come here? Quinn wondered before someone yelling at him to move out of their way pulled him out of his thoughts. He ran into the game again, shaking in head and deciding that it was not his business if the boy wanted to be a loner.

The game calmed down when the boys called quits and ended another round. Hozier, bounced the ball, staring at the ground as he asked a question, "Do any of you want to go to the pub? I heard there's a band playing there at eight."

Ever since Hozier became old enough to drink—eighteen—he'd been asking if anyone would like to follow him. Maybe there was something about getting a bottle while being old enough to have a drink that made him feel proud of himself. Half of the boys in grade twelve had turned eighteen, but a few people were still seventeen or even younger. It didn't matter though, as long as there were adults with them anyone above the age of sixteen was allowed to drink. The barkeeper didn't care much. There weren't that many adults in town to keep him in business anyway.

"I'll come," one of the boys said after a moment of brief silence. A few 'me too's rang in the group as a follow up to his response.

"Great!" Hozier said with a grin. He was wearing black converse and ripped jeans. He gave the others some details before turning his attention to Karl who was resting against the crisscross court gate. "How about you?"

"Nah, I can't come. I'm heading home with Quinn right after this," he said, wiping the sweat off his forehead. before looking down at Quinn who was crouched down under him and using him as a shade. It was six in the evening now, but it got dark fast, and the boys would have to end their game soon. They had come here right after school was out at two in the afternoon. Early—like it was every Friday.

"Yeah, that's true. Our mums want us home early. We promised," Quinn confirmed and Hozier nodded, combing back his blond hair with the fingers of his free hand. He was holding the basketball under his hand and would be taking it home with him for safekeeping.

"Maybe next time," Hozier said, and the two boys smiled.

"Of course," Quinn said as Hozier turned away and walked in the direction of the exit with the others. Quinn's gaze shifted to the stairs, wondering if the boy at the gate was still there, but just like always he had disappeared before the group had called it a day.

He sighed, looking up. "Ready to leave?" Quinn asked Karl whose eyes were now darting around the court. He might have lost a sock or something. Their basketball games got so heated that clothes started coming off—mostly shoes and shirts. Yes, but sometimes they did end up playing in just underwear after drenching their shorts and pants in too much sweat.

Karl didn't answer Quinn right away, he made a beeline for the piece of fabric at the end of the court. He picked it up before looking back at Quinn. "I am now!" He said, waving the blue sock in his hand. Quinn laughed, getting up before walking up to Karl.

The two left the court together and started to make their way home, humming pop songs as the soles of their worn-out converse shoes crushed the grains of sand under their feet. It was approaching summer, and it was getting hotter and drier with every passing day.

"What was on your mind this afternoon? You were absent-minded. In fact, you've been this way for a few weeks mate," Karl said out of the blue, making Quinn turn to face him before looking up ahead and shrugging. The orange light the roads had been drowned in had now given way to a dull blue-yellow as time went beyond seven in the evening.

"It's nothing really. Why have you been looking at me, though?" Quinn asked, raising a suggestive brow at Karl. His friend rolled his eyes before giving his shoulder a small shove.

"It's hard not to when you keep getting hit by the basketball," Karl said.

"You just didn't!" Quinn said, and his eyes went wide. He shoved Karl back, and Karl did it again. The two laughed, chasing each other in the evening, and stopping their dumb chase when they got to the street they lived on.

The buildings on this side of town were tightly packed and old. The street lights didn't work, so it was a good idea to always head home early. Quinn and Karl didn't live two far from each other. In fact, they lived in the same complex and their apartments were just a few doors apart.

The two head into the rundown building they lived in and took the stairs to the sixth floor since the elevators had been jammed since last week.

"See you later," Karl said, tapping Quinn's shoulder before heading towards the door to his family's apartment.

"You too," Quinn said, watching Karl disappear. He didn't turn towards his own apartment until the lock to Karl's door creaked shut.

Quinn opened the door, before heading in and closing the door behind him. There was no mudroom. The door led straight into the kitchenette that shared a space with the small living room. Quinn walked about, checking the corridor that led to the rooms to see if anyone was around, but the lights weren't on and there was no one in sight.

"Huh, they're not back. Isn't it seven yet?" Quinn wondered out loud. He decided not to think too much about it, his parents and sister were probably working late. He instead headed to his own room that was at the end of the hallway. He opened the door, walking in before flipping the light switch and letting the yellow fluorescence light flood the room in its glow. It was a small place. The two ends of the twin bed he had touched both ends of the wall. There wasn't much space for anything else, but Quinn had managed to fit in a small drawer for his clothes.

Quinn took off his shirt, before getting out of his jogging pants. He hopped into a loose pair of shorts before climbing into bed. As he stared out into his room images of the dark-haired boy sitting at the stairs of the gates flooded his mind.

Who is he? He asked himself, frowning a bit as he tried to jog his memory for any clues. The boy often wore loose pants and cheap cotton slogan t-shirts. It's been over a month since he had started to sit at the gates to the basketball court. Quinn and his friends played at the court very evening they could, and the boy was always present at the stairs—at least for the past few weeks. He never walked up to them to ask to join. He just sat at the stairs by himself, and rarely ever turned to look at anybody. Since Quinn started to pay attention to him, he noticed the boy would appear in the middle of a game, and then disappear just before he and his friends started to leave the court.

Quinn couldn't put a finger on who he was, but he had to be a student at their school. It was a small town, and there wasn't another high school for miles to come.

Maybe he's new? Quinn wondered. Everyone in town often knew everyone else. It was a small community of about eight hundred people at most. They shared the same school and church, and everyone shopped at the same grocery, thrift, and convenience stores.

Maybe I should ask around? Quinn wondered, turning until his brown eyes were fixated on the ceiling about. He was in his last year of high school, and it was possible the boy was someone in a different class or even a different grade.

Maybe he's a junior? Maybe even a sophomore? He continued to guess, letting out a sigh.

Quinn listened to the sound of his wall clock tick as he kept thinking. From time to time, his eyes will flicker to the posters he had up in his room. He sat up at a point, rubbing the space between his brows to try and relax the frown he had been wearing since he stepped into his room. Not knowing who that boy was bothered him. He wondered if he should approach him next time, maybe ask him to play a game with them?

"Fuck," Quinn let out, flipping back into his bed before shutting his eyes close to get the image of the strange boy out of his head.

CHAPTER TWO

It was early in the evening, and the sun was already retreating behind the clouds. Quinn walked around the basketball court alone, bouncing the ball on the clay floor, and catching it when it hit his waiting palms. The rest of the boys couldn't make it today. They had other things to do—namely, cleaning duty because they laughed at a teacher earlier in the day. So, Quinn came by himself, borrowing the ball from Hozier so he could shoot some hoops by himself. The boys had promised to come over if they finished early, but it was already five-thirty in the afternoon and Quinn had to be back home before the clock hit six.

A sigh left Quinn's lips as stood still. He was still in the dark blue trousers and flannel top he had worn to school in the morning. The boys would usually change into something comfortable in the school's bathroom before heading to the court, but there was no use for that today since he was in a one-man game today.

Quinn looked up at the raised basket post in front of him before tossing the ball. It flew through the air, hitting the side of the rusty ring before bouncing off and hitting the ground. The sound of the ball rolling halfway through the court was the only noise that flooded the background. Quinn watched the ball roll, but his head snapped in the direction of the court's exit when he heard the aluminum gates rustle.

"Hello?" Quinn called out when the rustling stopped. He frowned. "Hello, is someone there?" A frown played on his face, and his eyes stayed fixed on the gates.

"If someone is out there just come out. We can share the basketball if you want. You don't have to hide." Quinn wasn't sure why he had said that. If it was who he thought it was the boy wouldn't buy into that. He kept staring at the gates, but nothing happened. With a sigh, he turned away, heading to pick up the basketball before continuing his solo match with himself.

Quinn wondered if someone was there, or if his mind had just been playing games with him. He'd been jumpy for the past week. His mind becoming more and more preoccupied with the small dark-haired boy he'd spot watching him and his mates. He had looked around his school and had even asked a few people outside his grade about the person. His descriptions of him had been messy, so it wasn't a surprise he hadn't gone very far in his search the past week. It was Thursday now. He still had Friday to ask around, and if he didn't get any answers Quinn promised to stop looking.

A sigh left his lips before he groaned. As he was about to credit the sound to his head tricking him the gates rustled again. Quinn turned, waiting to see if someone would walk in, but nobody did. He bit down on his bottom lip, feeling a bit frustrated. "If someone's there, just come out," he said as his heartbeat quickened with excitement. His grip on the battered ball he had in his hands tightened and his gaze stayed fixed on the aluminum gates.

Nothing.

Quinn was beginning to wonder if it was the wind, but it couldn't be. It was early in the summer and the tree leaves and branches barely moved.

"If you're not coming out. I'll come to get you," he said, getting frustrated with his hide and seek game.

At Quinn's words, a boy—the boy who'd always observed them walked from behind the bushes and just stood at the stairs behind the gates with wide eyes. The threat had worked. Quinn could tell the boy was afraid by the way he was shaking. Quinn blinked, feeling his face warm-up at the boy's sight. He said what he had out of frustration. He never thought the boy would show himself because of that.

He stared at the boy's pale skin and big brown eyes. His dark hair was longish and stopped at the nape of his neck where it folded into curls. He wore what he always did. A pair of baggy pants and a logo t-shirt. Like Quinn had guessed he looked a bit younger than himself. He looked maybe sixteen or seventeen. He could be older, and the doe eyes and round face might be why he looked younger. Quinn couldn't tell.

There was pin-drop silence as the two boys observed each other for the next few minutes. Quinn's heart couldn't stop racing. Finally, he'd met the boy.

Quinn let out a breath as his shoulder's sagged. "You're quite the peeping tom—"

"No!" The boy yelled, shocking Quinn. The boy looked just as shocked at his outburst. "I'm sorry. I..." he trailed, looking down at the clay floor before bringing his thumb to his lips to nibble on its nail.

Quinn raised a brow in surprise, wondering what the blushing mess in front of him was about. The boy had an oddly deep voice for his size. You wouldn't pair him with his own voice if you were blindfolded and ask to pick via touch alone in a line-up. He was small and skinny. He was shorter than Quinn, and Quinn wasn't even very tall himself.

"What do you mean, no? I see you looking at me and my friends every other day. Of course, you're a peeping Tom," Quinn said with a light laugh. He stared at the boy, who didn't seem amused at Quinn's teasing. The boy hugged himself and had his eyes fixated on the floor as he stays quiet.

"Why didn't you ever just walk into the court to play with us?" Quinn asked after a while of silence. He watched as the boy shrugged before holding on to the railing of the court's gate. His knuckles were white—not just because his skin was pale, but also because it was dry.

A sigh left Quinn's lips as he rolled the basketball in his hands. "You don't plan to say anything, do you?" he said and watched as the boy nodded in response.

"Suit yourself," Quinn said with a shrug, turning around before returning to his one-man game. If the boy wanted to stare at him forever, he could go ahead.

As Quinn continued to play on the court, he noticed that the dark-haired boy had made to sit on the stairs by the gate again. He wasn't sure how he felt about being watched, so he just continued bouncing the ball on the clay floor and making tosses at the baskets. He wondered what and the rest were doing. Sure, they were serving a punishment, but cleaning around the school compound while you joked with friends wasn't as bad as being alone as he was.

A sigh left Quinn's lips as he paused his game. He held the basketball under one arm before heading to grab his school bag he had put in the corner. Quinn looked out into the court one last time before turning to face the gates again. "Can I at least get your name?" he asked, waiting for the boy to respond.

There was some hesitance before the boy nodded. "Cody," he said, his voice small and shaky.

"Cody," Quinn said, repeating after him. He liked the name, and he felt it suited him. Quinn smiled, nodding to himself. "So, see you around Cody," he said, walking towards the gates. Cody scooted to the side of the stairs so that Quinn could pass. It was the closest they'd been to each other, and Quinn found himself taking a closer look at him from the side of his eyes. He had nice bow lips, but they were dry and cracked. His eyebrows were hidden under his fringe, and his collarbones popped from under his shirt. He looked so fragile, and Quinn found himself frozen on the stairs, not wanting to leave him by himself.

"Your name?" The sound of Cody's voice snapped him out of his staring trance.

"M-my what?" he asked, stuttering in embarrassment and blinking back a few times before fixing his gaze on Cody. He had spaced out and hadn't caught Cody's words.

"What's your name?" Cody asked again. His deep voice had gone soft and light, and Quinn was just able to catch what he said this time.

"Oh, it's Quinn," he said, making Cody frown a bit.

"Queen?" the frail boy asked, watching as Quinn frowned at him before groaning.

"No, it's Quinn." He emphasized the slight difference in pronunciation, making Cody nod.

"Oh, I get it," he said. Quinn didn't say anything in response, but he didn't walk away either. The two stayed by in the gate and were soon plunged into silence.

"Is it short for anything?" Cody asked after a bit, getting a bit uncomfortable with the silence.

"It's Quinn. Just call me Quinn." Quinn knew his voice was too firm, but he wasn't giving anyone his full name, and definitely not to some person he just met. Quinn was short for Quincy, and Quinn hated his full name with a burning passion.

"Okay..." Cody croaked; a bit creeped out by Quinn's little outburst. The silence returned, and it was more uncomfortable than the last spell.

Quinn felt bad, and he wanted to get away from the situation. He starts walking away but stops in his tracks when he gets to the last stair. "You live around here, right?" he asked, turning to face Cody.

"Yeah, I moved in with my mum a while back," Cody muttered under his breath as he played with his fingers.

So, I was right. Quinn thought to himself. He's new here.

"Ah, okay. If you ever need someone to show you around, you know where to find me," Quinn offered, rubbing the back of his neck with his free hand.

Cody smiled, shocking Quinn a bit. The skinny boy licked his lips before looking past him. "Thank you," he said, nibbling the nail of his thumb again as he made eye contact with Quinn. The two stared at each other for a bit, and Quinn only looked away when he started to feel his cheeks grow warm.

"I'll get going..." he trailed, looking away from Cody before speed walking towards the main street. His heart was racing from the mundane interaction, and Quinn couldn't understand why.

CHAPTER THREE

Tamworth's high school was a multipurpose school building. It also housed the middle schoolers, as well as the kids in grade school and kindergarten. It was an old mall building that had been renovated to what was now the school. It still felt like a mall in many ways, mostly because of all the open space between classrooms.

In one of the rundown classrooms in the local high school's section of the building, most of the desks were vandalized and wobbly, and most seats had to be sat on carefully so that they wouldn't fall apart. It was the break before the last class period, and Quinn was sitting at the right of the classroom with some of his friends.

Karl was sitting on one of the desks. He looked out into the room for a bit and groaned, catching the attention of his friends. "Seems like she's heading towards us," he simply said. Everyone knew who 'she' was, so they groaned too, sighing amongst themselves.

Quinn looked up from the Rubix cube he was playing with, before looking out into the classroom to see what the fuss was about, and just like Karl said, 'she' was heading their way.

Lindsey.

"Not her again," Quinn mumbled under his breath, making his friends laugh at his discomfort.

Lindsey was a special case. She had a crush on Quinn and found a way to pester him all day, and the break period was, unfortunately, a very good period for her to do that.

The girl soon stopped in front of Quinn's desk. There was a smile on her face like she hadn't realized all the commotion at the corner was about her arrival.

"Hello!" she said, with a toothy grin, climbing onto the desk Quinn was sitting by. Quinn felt the bile rise in his throat. She smelled like fruit and flowers. He didn't like the way girls in his class smelled. He didn't like it at all.

"Hey." Quinn managed to return the greeting as his shoulders slumped. He didn't want to do this push-pull ordeal with Lindsey during the break period.

"So, what are you up to?" the girl asked, crossing her legs and twisting one of her many colorful braids she had adorned in beads between her fingers. The class was noisy, but Lindsey was too close for Quinn to pretend like he didn't hear her.

Quinn was now playing with his Rubric cube again. "Nothing really," he muttered, making Lindsey laugh awkwardly before looking away from him.

"But you're playing with a Rubix cube. That's something." Linsey pointed out, leaning so close to Quinn that he shuddered.

Quinn sighed under his breath. "I guess it is."

Time passed by, and Quinn continues to answer Lindsey's questions with dry short sentences. Most people would have left after they'd figured out that they were not wanted, but Lindsey stayed. Her crush on the bronze-skinned boy with bright brown eyes made her perch around like an unwanted hummingbird.

"The break is over, bring out the essay assignment I gave to you last week. I don't want to hear an excuse as to why you don't have them, so if any of you were planning to talk to me, forget it and accept your zero." The break ended with the history teacher bursting through the doors, making most of the kids in class grumble as they got of desks and seats before heading to their rightful positions in class.

Lindsey left too, but not without a little hesitance. She tried to get Karl to swap seats with her, but when that didn't work, she accepted her fate and hopped off Quinn's desk before heading to her seat.

"Finally," Karl said, settling down beside Quinn. Quinn smiled, chuckling a bit. His good mood was back.

The class was boring as usual. The teacher was a grey-haired man that was in his early fifties to mid-fifties. Quinn spent most of the class time doodling in his notebook, and Karl exchanged texts with someone by hiding his phone under the desk. The class ended at three in the afternoon, marking the end of the school day.

"Wait up!"

Quinn turned at the sound of Lindsey calling out to him. She grinned, slipping past the crowd of students making it to the door, before stopping in front of him.

"What do you want?" Quinn asked, frowning a bit. Most of the students were gone, and now it was just him. He knew at least Karl would wait for him at the school's main exit, but he didn't want to be here alone with Lindsey.

"I want to tell you something," Lindsey said, clamping her hands together in front of her. She was wearing a loose-fitting yellow top over a fitted midi-skirt that was just above her knees.

"Okay, go ahead," Quinn said, being as cold to her as usual.

That didn't faze Lindsey. She was used to it. "I like you," she said after looking around to find that the class was empty. "I really like you," she emphasized, not wanting to give Quinn the opportunity to pretend as if he didn't understand her.

However, Quinn did it anyway. "I think you're cool too," he said, looking past her shoulders in an attempt not to stare into her eyes. She was making him uncomfortable, but he wasn't one to push someone away.

"No, I like you. As in, romantically. I want us to hang out. I want us to date," Lindsey said as her lips quiver. Quinn was trying to push her aside, but she wasn't going to let him do it without a fight. There. She had said it plainly. He couldn't pretend to be oblivious to her feelings now.

"Oh," Quinn let out, feeling uncomfortable. He rubbed the back of his neck before looking out at the window. He spotted Hozier's tall figure and he felt a bit better. If Hozier was waiting for him, so was Karl. The other boy wasn't just tall enough to be spotted through the window.

"Is that all you have to say?" Irritation was clear in Lindsey's tone. "Oh?"

"Yeah, I guess," Quinn said, looking down at his mud-stained sneakers. They had done some track during P.E. today, and the tracks were just leveled ground with chalk used to draw in the separation lines.

A sigh left Lindsey's lips as her shoulder's slumped. "Think about it," she said before sucking in her lip. "I'll talk to you tomorrow," she added, touching Quinn's shoulder before walking past him and out the classroom door.

Quinn didn't turn his back until the door to the classroom shut, telling him that Lindsey had left. He leet out a sigh, biting his thumbnail as he made his way out of the classroom as well. There was something about girls that jarred him and made him uncomfortable when they expressed interest in him. Usually, they stopped bugging him when he didn't show any interest back, but Lindsey had a lot of perseverance.

"What was she going on about?" Hozier asked when Quinn met them at the classroom's window.

"Stuff," Quinn said, not wanting to talk about it. Hozier rose a brow at him, and Karl just chuckled, shaking his head. The two knew Quinn was the socially awkward one when it came to girls. He dodged them like they were bullets, and they had no doubt that Quinn would do the same to Lindsey.

"Why do they keep asking you out? Why doesn't a girl like Lindsey talk to me?" Hozier sighed as the group started to make their way out of the school compound.

"Well, maybe because Quinn's the best looking, and good looking girls like good looking guys, it's not science." Karl offered. The three were heading to the basketball court. It was a fifteen-minute walk, give or take.

"Well, that's shallow," Hozier groaned. There was no argument over if Quinn was the best looking. He was. Well, at least based on what was popular with the girls at their school. Living in a small impoverished town meant that people opted to watch Latin and Spanish dramas since you could rent them from Bobby at the thrift store. Quinn was one of the few boys in town that matched the descriptions of the 'Gaels' and 'Pablos' on television.

Karl rolled his eyes. "You're shallow too. You only want Linsey to ask you out because she's hot."

"Fair," Hozier said with a grin that exposed his buck teeth. All three of the boys were already loose pants and loose-fitting tops since they'd had a gym session earlier in the school day.

"Can we talk about something else?" Quinn asked, making his friends pause their bickering. It didn't last, though.

"With the way you avoid girls I'd think you were hiding something from us," Hozier said, ignoring Quinn's request. "Are you gay, lad?" he asked with a chuckle, and Kar laughed too, moving to grab Quinn's shoulder before pulling him into a side hug.

"It wouldn't matter if you were. Ignore him," Karl said, and Quinn stayed quiet, unamused.

Although Quinn was brooding like he did when Hozier made jabs like that, there was something different about this time. Usually, when his friends made the 'gay' joke he'd just be slightly annoyed, but now his mind was just filled with images of Cody. The lean boy with pale skin and husky voice that clashed with his frame.

Quinn sucked on his teeth, jogging his thoughts for an explanation as to why he was feeling the way he did. It's been this way for the past few days. Cody still sat by the gates during Quinn's games with his friends and it made Quinn self-conscious. Quinn didn't know Cody very well. He had talked to him once, and Quinn wouldn't call what had transpired a proper conversation pe say.

Odd, Quinn thought to himself. The voices of his friends turned into a light background buzz as he tuned them out and focused on the images of Cody in his head. He hoped he would be at the court already.

CHAPTER FOUR

Quinn was at the basketball court late after the game had ended. Cody had not come this afternoon. At first, Quinn had wanted to leave with his friends, but something in him compelled him to stay. Maybe Cody was late today and would still drop by.

Dummy. Quinn scolded himself in his head as he kept making baskets as he walks about the court thinking to himself. He wondered why he was so worried that Cody hadn't come to watch them today. He wondered why he cared so much, but nothing could answer his questions. The trees growing around the fenced-off court had left leaves on the clay surface, and the scorching hot sun had retreated into the clouds to allow for a cool blue-washed. The dimness meant it was harder to make baskets, and Quinn had to squint whenever he threw the ball from a good distance away.

As Quinn bounced the ball and moved around the court, his mind moved to Lindsey. What to do. He wondered as he tried to come up with the kindest way possible to turn her down. Lindsey wasn't like the other girls that had come up to him before. She would make some noise and draw attention to herself if she was rejected.

The sound of the court gates rattling pull Quinn out of his thoughts. He holds on to the basketball and turns on his heels to face the aluminum gates.

"Oh, it's you." Quinn tried to make his voice come off as uninterested, but some of his excitement at seeing Cody had snuck in, making his voice higher. He smiled, staring at the lean boy who pushed the gates open before stepping into the court.

"You're here alone again," Cody said to Quinn, making him shrug his shoulders. Quinn turned around, throwing the ball in his hands before watching it pass through the hoop. The ball bounces about when it hits the clay ground before rolling over to Quinn who picks it up.

"And you're still being a peeping Tom. Nothing's quite new, is it?" Quinn said, laughing to himself.

Cody walks into Quinn's view, and this time he was smiling at Quinn's joke. The two boys didn't say anything, and the sound of the ball hitting the clay floor as Quinn made it bounce on the spot was the only sound drowning the background.

"So, do you play?" Quinn asked after a while.

"No, but I can try," Cody said, looking over at Quinn. The darker boy takes a few steps back, making Cody raise a brown at him.

Okay then, give it a shot," Quinn said, throwing the ball at Cody before the boy could ask any questions.

"Ah, fuck. I told you I could try, not that I could," Cody said, jumping away from the ball before heading over to pick it up. Quinn found himself fixated on the fact the boy had cursed. For some reason, he hadn't pinned him as one to do that.

"Throw it back," Quinn said, gesturing to himself, and Cody did just that. Quin caught the ball, before rolling it between his hands. "Let's bounce it back and forth," he said as he tossed the ball to the ground, making it bounce off the clay floor before heading for Cody. The boy caught it this time, and soon they had formed a nice back and forth pass.

The sound of the ball bouncing on the clay floor echoed through the court as the boys remained silent.

Quinn felt the need to talk, so he started a conversation. "So, why are you always here?" he asked, letting out the question he'd had in his head for the past two months.

Cody shrugged, passing the ball. "I don't know. I randomly left home and kind of found you guys playing basketball after a while of wandering. I liked watching, so I just come here to watch you guys now to ease my boredom if that makes sense."

"I see," Quinn said.

Cody let out a low sigh. "I don't like being at home, really."

"Why?" Quinn asked with a frown before holding on to the ball and stopping the game of pass.

"I don't want to talk about it," Cody said, and Quinn just nodded. The silence that followed was uncomfortable, and Quinn found himself staring down at his dirted converse shoes.

"So, what are you doing here all by yourself today?" Cody asked, making Quinn raise his head.

His face warmed up. He couldn't bring himself to tell Cody that he waited for him, so he told him a half-truth instead. "I came to think about something, really. I'm trying to decide on what to do, he said, referring to his issue with Lindsey.

"Is it about something serious?" Cody asked, making Quinn bite down on his bottom lip.

"No, not really. There's this girl I have to let down. I'm not sure how to tell her," Quinn said, running a hand through his dark hair.

Cody nodded. "Oh, that kind of problem," the boy said, stuffing his hands into the pocket of his baggy jeans.

Quinn smiled, chuckling a bit. "Do you have any advice for me?"

Cody shook his head. "I'm not good with girls. No one thinks I'm attractive anyway, so I'm kind of lucky not to have those problems?" His last sentence came off as a question, and Quinn wasn't sure what to say to that so he just smiled, mirroring the awkward grin on the pale boy's face.

Quinn hated it when people made self-deprecating comments. It didn't just sit well with him. Also, Cody was attractive. Well, to Quinn. He had that cute shy look going on for him. His face grew warm when he noticed he was staring at Cody. He looked away, jogging his mind for something to say in response.

"I guess you just have to be honest with her really. I'm not sure what else to say. Then again, I'm not the best source of advice for this," Cody muttered after some time passed, chuckling to himself.

"Yeah, that's what I'm planning to do. I don't want to be mean about it, you know?" Quinn said, feeling better. It was nice to talk to someone about this. His friends would just go on about how lucky he was and wouldn't answer any of his questions.

"You look like a cold-hearted person, but you ooze of kindness if that makes sense. It's quite a shock," Cody said out of the blue, making Quinn look up at him with a grin.

"Oh really?" Quinn asked. He wasn't sure why the compliment made him so happy, but it did.

Cody nodded, smiling a bit. "The first time you caught me looking, I thought you'd come right over to punch me or something," Cody said, letting out a light laugh.

"Oh, do I look mean?" Quinn asked, feeling self-conscious.

"I'm not sure. You have a resting bitch face of some sort, but it's okay," Cody said, hugging himself. Quinn laughed, and the basketball court fell back into silence.

"Why didn't you ask to join us, though?" Quinn asked after a while, not wanting the conversation to die.

"I can't play basketball," Cody said, staring at the ball Quinn now had tucked under his arm. "I also fuck friendships up a lot. I don't think I'm ready for any of that now," Cody added, making Quinn curious.

"Is that so?" Quinn asked.

Cody sighed, "yeah."

There was another pause that only ended when Quinn spoke up.

"We're friends, though? I think we're friends," he said, making Cody's doe brown eyes widen.

"Oh." The smaller boy let out, scratching the back of his neck.

"Don't you think we are?" Quinn asked, and Cody seemed to had been taken aback.

"We've talked, and we're even playing basketball together," Quinn added. He wasn't sure why he wanted Cody to consider him as a friend, but he knew he did. The pale boy nibbled on his bottom lip, darting his eyes from one end of the court to the other as his mouth parted a bit.

"I—" he started but shook his head. "Yeah, we are," he said instead and Quinn smiled at him, starting up the game of pass again.

Quinn continued to talk with Cody about Lindsey and his friends they passed the ball amongst themselves.

"Your friends drink?" Cody asked when Quinn talked about Hozier vomiting his heart out after a trip to the bar.

"Yeah, they're old enough to," Quinn said, making Cody nod.

"Do you drink?" Cody asked, and Quinn blinked, looking straight at him before passing the ball back to the smaller boy. He wasn't sure why, but a bit of him wanted to lie about that. Maybe Cody didn't like drinking? But why in the world should Quinn care what he thought about it?

Quinn shook his head, deciding to be honest. "Sometimes, not too much though."

"Oh, okay," Cody muttered, tossing the ball back.

Cody wasn't very open about himself. He listened to Quinn's stories, but whenever the darker boy asked him something personal, he seemed to recoil into himself a bit, so Quinn stopped asking. Instead, he asked him about the food and music he liked, and suddenly Cody had a lot to say. The boy's childish excitement surrounding his favorite indie bands was 'wholesome' as Quinn's inner voice put it.

After an hour or so they stopped playing and Quinn put the ball under his arm before telling Cody he had to leave. It was about eight in the evening now, and the only thing lighting up the court was the moon and the night post stationed a few meters away from the court.

"Goodbye then." Cody smiled as Quinn went ahead to grab his bag before making his way towards the gate.

Quinn turned to grin at Cody. "See you later peeping Tom," he said, making Cody laugh and roll his eyes.

There was something about the boy's laugh that made Quinn's chest squeeze up and his stomach flutter. He wanted to ask if Cody would like to walk home together, but he looked away quickly instead, making a run for it before his dumb thoughts could put him in trouble.

CHAPTER FIVE

T he school day was over, and most students had made their way to the school's compound where they talked to their friends as the crowd thinned with time. The sun was harsh, so most people were by the school's brick walls, trying to take shade under the small bit of roofing that curved over the building's walls. Quinn was with a group of his friends. They were talking by the school entrance.

"Hey! How are you?" A voice said, rising above the voice of the other students in the front yard.

Quinn looked up, finding Lindsey making her way to his group of friends. She had an expectant grin on her face. She stopped in front of Quinn, making his friends back away to give them space.

"Oh. Hey Lindsey..." Quinn muttered, not matching her enthusiasm. He ran a hand through his hair as his gaze flickered to the dirt floor. She hadn't spoken to him in days, and he had falsely believed that maybe she had stopped wanting to date him.

Here we go again. Quinn thought to himself when Lindsey moves a little too close. Her perfume made him feel a bit nauseous, and Quinn wanted to leave. His friends could see he was uncomfortable, but no one got in the middle of a love quarrel. They even elected to give the two more space, by wandering even further away from them.

Lindsey leans into Quinn's face. "Can we talk now?" Her voice fans Quinn's ear in a low tone, making him quiver.

"Sure..." he trailed, watching as the girl smiled before taking his hand and pulling him along with her. The two of them walk off to the other corner of the wall together. Quinn put his hands in his pocket before staring down at the floor, while Lindsey crossed her skinny hands over her small chest.

"So?" she started, breaking the silence between them. Quinn looks up at her, gauging the expectant look on her face.

"So, what?" he ended up asking, making Lindsey let out a sigh before rolling her eyes. She turned, resting her back on the red brick wall before looking out into the school compound.

"Acting like you're oblivious is getting old. I'm not sure whether you think it's cute, but it's not. I'm asking about what I asked you to think about. Will you give me a chance? We can go for a date and you can decide then." Lindsey said, making Quinn look away before running his fingers through his hair.

"Lindsey..." Quinn trailed, not finding the heart to reject her out flat. He wondered if she would take it well, and that made him nervous. situations like this always made him nervous.

Lindsey frowned at him. "What? Don't keep me waiting," she said, leaning off the wall. "What is it? Say something."

"I'm not interested, I'm sorry." Quinn managed to blurt. He watched as the frown on Lindsey's face shifted from one of hurt to anger in the span of seconds.

"So, it's true," she muttered under her breath—her voice just high enough for Quinn to catch it. She held on to the sides of her face, closing her eyes before cursing under her breath.

"What's wrong?" Quinn asked, stepping forward.

"So, it's true that you're gay," Lindsey said, opening her eyes. Quinn felt light a bucket of cold water had been poured on him. He didn't say anything, and Lindsey considered that proof that her snitch was true.

"I mean, it makes sense. You won't date me, you won't date any other girl, and look at you..." she trailed, motioning towards his appearance. "You're good looking. Are you telling me that you've not even considered dating? Not even once? Even with the number of people that approach you?"

"I—" Quinn started, but he couldn't find the words to say. "I have thought of dating some people, it's just..." he trailed, squeezing his hands into fists before casting his gaze to the ground again. The words coming out of his mouth didn't sound right. If Quinn had to be honest to himself, he'd never thought of dating anyone at all. His life had been mostly friends, sports, and home. Although his friends talked about the dates they were going to or the people they'd laid, the whole discussion had always felt annoying to Quinn—sometimes even gross.

"Sure, I believe you," Lindsey chuckled. Her tone was jeering—stained with sarcasm. The two stayed within distance for the next few minutes. After a while of silence, Lindsey huffed before walking away. Quinn watched her disappear into the crowd before sighing and walking back to his group of friends.

"How did it go?" Hozier asked when Quinn was within earshot.

"I guess she was a little pissed," Quinn said, and his pals laughed before going back to the conversation they'd been having about an animation show before Quinn showed up. They hung around the front yard, changing their discussion topic from time to time. Quinn couldn't follow any of it. His mind was buzzing from his interaction with Lindsey, and he felt numb all over—and a bit like he had been aired out in the sun to dry.

Despite that, he followed the group to the basketball when they decided to leave the school premises. The school compound was empty now, and freshmen might have gotten to the court before them. It didn't matter. They were seniors, so they didn't have to worry about anyone being in there. If a group of kids had made it there before them, all they had to do was tell them to leave.

They did just that when they got there, apologizing to the youngers as they replaced them on the court. A game started soon after, and Quinn couldn't focus. He kept thinking about Lindsey.

About what she had said.

Was he gay? Was that why he kept worrying about Cody?

Karl gave Quinn's shoulder a light punch. "Stay with us, man. You're always drifting off," he said, making the two other lads passing him in the court laugh.

"I'm sorry," Quinn muttered under his breath, holding on to his head. No one responded to his apology since all was forgotten instantly and the game continued around him.

At a point, Karl noticed that Quinn was drifting off again. He rolled his eyes before tossing the ball in the direction of his friend. Quinn seemed to have jogged out of the musing in his head himself before he gets hit because he caught the ball mid-air. There was a roar of clapping as he dribbled it on the court, causing the game of disorganized basketball to continue.

Throughout the match Quinn found himself looking over at the bushes by the side of the rusty court gates, but he never spotted Cody. A feeling of disappointment mixed with worry consumed him, and he couldn't mask it properly. It caused his friends to ask him if he was okay from time to time as they bumped into him while dribbling and running around.

"Are you okay?" Hozier asked. He had come up to Quinn immediately after the match had ended. It was late in the evening now, and the warm orange glow from earlier in the day had faded to a yellow-blue. Quinn looked up. He had sweat dripping from his face as he heaved. He was bent over, trying to catch his breath. He'd got back in his senses in the second half, but Hozier had still noticed some oddness so he came to ask himself.

Quinn let out a sigh. "I'm fine," he said, stretching. His shirt rode-up his torso due to the action. He looked away from Hozier before cleaning the sweat off his face with his shirt and combing his hair with his fingers.

"Well, you don't look like you are," Hozier said, still probing. Yeah, some days Quinn was off, but his lack of concentration had been going on for the stretch of two months. He switches the basketball from under one arm to the other, watching as Quinn picked up his bag before standing up straight and sighing.

"I'm fine," Quinn repeated, walking past Hozier. Their shoulder's pushed, and there was a tension Quinn knew he would have to resolve later.

The group of boys walked home together, and people stopped at their individual houses as they continued their journey. Soon enough it was just Karl and Quinn by themselves. The two boys walked together in silence. Quinn wasn't in the mood to talk about anything, and Karl didn't want to be the one to poke at the brooding lad. They got to the apartment complex where their homes were before heading up the stairs for the sixth floor.

When the two were standing by their doors Karl decided he had to say something.

"If something's bothering you can tell me," he said, holding on to the handle of his apartment door. There was the sound of a buzzing T.V. in the hallway. The walls were thin in the building.

Quinn let out a sigh before smiling. "Thanks for worrying about me, but I'm fine. I promise." He insisted.

Karl didn't believe him, but he didn't want to confront him in a way that would lead to a fight in the hallway. "If you say so," he said instead, smiling a bit before opening the door to his apartment and walking in. Quinn let out a sigh and covered his face with his hand when Karl's door closed behind him.

He turned, opening the door to his apartment before walking in and closing it behind him.

As Quinn got around to taking a shower and changing, he continued to wonder where Cody had been today. He wondered if the boy was sick, or if he had just grown tired of watching him and his friends play basketball.

For some reason that last thought made Quinn feel a bit depressed.

Why does that bother me? Quinn asked himself as he climbed into his bed before lying down like a starfish and staring up at the ceiling. For the first time in forever, a bit part of his day was getting occupied by the thoughts of someone other than himself.

CHAPTER SIX

- -

A little convenience store was located at the center of the small town. Like everything else in the town and its neighborhood, it was old, rundown, and badly managed. Nevertheless, it offered snacks and comic books, and was it was well-loved by students who wanted to grab something on their way home.

It was early in the evening on a Thursday, and Quinn had split from his group of friends in other to get a drink. When Quinn walked in, he strolled through the store a bit, surprised to find the person he's been looking out for the past week. Cody was in the store, standing at a nearby aisle and looking through the small comic section the store had.

Where have you been? The question was at Quinn's tongue. He wanted to run over to Cody and shake him by the shoulders for disappearing into thin air, but they weren't that close for him to be that upset. Quinn stood still, not knowing what to do. It was the first time he had seen Cody in over a week, and just when he had told himself he would try to stop thinking about him the small boy reappeared—doe eyes and baby face intact. With a deep breath, Quinn decides to approach him. He walks behind him, tapping his shoulder.

"Hey!" Quinn's voice was a bit shaky, even though he'd just wanted to sound friendly. It annoyed him. Why was he nervous?

Cody turned his head. His eyes were wide, but they went back to their normal size when he saw who it was.

"Oh, hey," his voice was low, and he didn't match Quinn's enthusiasm at all. Quinn started to feel nervous. Maybe Cody didn't want him there. He contemplated making an excuse to leave, but he pushed himself, deciding to continue the conversation.

"So, what are you doing?" Quinn asked after a bit, letting go of Cody's shoulder before tucking it into his jean pocket. Stupid. He scolded himself, squeezing his hand in his pocket. He touched his friends all the time, so why did his face feel warm and stomach twist up with nerves?

"I'm just looking around," Cody replied. The boy's face was blank, and he seemed oblivious to Quinn's inner turmoil. "Just looking," he repeated, staring at a row of comics. Quinn noticed the glint in his eyes, and he immediately reacted.

"Oh, you like comics?" Quinn asked, cocking his head at Cody who seemed to be avoiding his gaze.

"Yeah..." the boy trailed, running his hand through his dark hair. It was wild and flopped around his face. It didn't look like he had combed it in a while. It was a lot longer compared to the first time Quinn had seen him.

Quinn didn't say anything in response, so the conversation died, and the two boys stood in silence. Quinn wondered if he should just walk away, but a part of him didn't want to give up on talking to Quinn, so he kept going. "I came here to grab a pack of biscuits and a Pepsi. It's rather hot outside. Do you want anything? I could get it for you."

Cody frowned a bit, staring straight at Quinn with his deep brown eyes. "Do I want what?" The way Cody had asked the question shook Quinn a bit. He didn't seem interested at all, and Quinn was on the brink of apologizing and just leaving.

"Do you want a can of Pepsi or anything for that matter? I'll be paying, so don't worry," Quinn forced himself to say, suddenly feeling like Lindsey when she had kept bothering him. Did Cody think he was a bother? Was he acting weird? He didn't know, but what he did know was that he wanted to hang out with Cody. He hadn't seen him in a week, and if he slipped away now he wasn't sure where he'd find him.

Quinn watched as Cody's frown left and was replaced with a deep red blush that made Quinn's chest squeeze up. "Don't worry about it," Cody said, waving Quinn off before looking over the boy's shoulder.

"Come on now, don't hurt my feelings by rejecting my offer," Quinn said in a light-hearted joking way, but he meant it. Deep down the fact that Cody was saying 'no' hurt him and chipped at his confidence. He watched as Cody's face turned even redder as the boy fidgeted with his fingers.

"Why are you being so nice to me?"

I like you. The kneejerk reply to Cody's words in Quinn's head scared him, but he didn't budge. He was just grabbing Cody a drink. Friends did that. He and Cody were friends. "We're friends," he said, almost choking on his words when they left his mouth. It didn't feel right, but he needed a lie. He didn't want Cody to be weirded out by him.

Cody didn't ask any questions after that. He just looked at the ground before muttering, "can I have Pepsi?"

"Sure, I'll get that for you," Quinn said, turning and heading to the fridge, almost running judging by how quick he was walking. As he looked through the lineup of drinks Quinn wondered what to do with his feelings. He barely knew Cody, and how quickly he was growing attached to him both excited and scared him. A part of him thought that maybe he understood what his friends meant when they spoke about missing their girlfriends. A part of him was also starting to understand how quick some of his friends were to profess someone was good looking. He was starting to understand all these because he felt the same way about Cody. Maybe he was gay like Lindsey suggested, and knowing that brought him some relief. He wanted to understand himself further, and he wanted to explore the feelings he had for Cody.

There was a small barrier, though.

Okay, a big one.

Sure, they were both boys, but Quinn wasn't decided on whether he would express his feeling yet or if at all. Starting a friendship with Cody would be good for now. He could figure out the complexities of them both being of the same gender later.

A few minutes later Quinn and Cody met at the counter, and Quinn ended up paying for the snacks and the comic book Cody brought with him. He insisted it was fine when Cody tried to stop him, so the smaller boy had just watched on as Quinn exchanged money with the cashier. They left the convenience store together when Quinn got the bag of stuff they'd just purchased. They rested their backs on the walls, finding cover from the burning heat under the metal sheet roof that peaked past the store's brick walls.

"Here," Quinn said, fishing the bottle of Pepsi out of the black nylon bag he was holding before handing it to Cody who was quick to thank him.

"It's no problem," Quinn muttered, feeling his face burn. Their fingers had touched in the exchange, and now his heart was racing.

The boys stayed by the wall together, talking lightly as they both drank from their bottles of fizzy drinks. Their words were laced into short sentences and far between, but neither of them felt like the atmosphere was awkward. It felt comfortable in an oddly refreshing way.

Noticing the sun was retreating into the clouds, Quinn decided to make the face that he would leave soon heard. "I should be leaving soon. I'm supposed to help my mother move some things down to the apartment lobby, and the elevators aren't working." He looked at Cody who hadn't reacted. The boy's eyes were focused on the streets ahead. "Do you live around here?" Quinn asked out of the blue, making Cody blink before staring at him with wide eyes.

"Yeah, I do," he said, looking away from Quinn, and focusing on the now empty bottle in his hand.

"Great, do you want to walk back together?" he asked, getting excited.

Cody shook his head. "No."

Quinn felt his blood drain at the short rejection. "Why not?"

Cody remained quiet, and Quinn felt bad. A no was a no, he shouldn't have been quick to push for reasons.

Quinn let out a sigh before. "Okay then, see you later I guess," he said, before stretching his hand holding the nylon bag to Cody. It had the snacks and comic book he'd gotten for him. "Don't forget this," he said.

Cody thanked Quinn, taking the bag from him before watching the older boy walk away.

A fond smile played on Cody's face after Quinn left. The boy sighed, turning the can of empty Pepsi in his hands one last time before crushing it and tossing it into the nearby trash can. He bit his bottom lip as he felt his jean pocket for the paperback comic he'd folded and put there. He stared at it, flipping through the pages and still feeling warm in the chest at Quinn's gesture of kindness.

There'd been a high chance that Cody might have taken it out of the shelves and found a way to slip through the door without being unnoticed, but Quinn had come around and paid for it.

The smile on Cody's face was starting to feel a bit painful. He put the comic away, touching his lips as his hand with the nylon bag of snacks swung a bit in his grip. Quinn had not been the huge bully he'd thought him to be just from appearances. He seemed rather nice—good-willed—and a tad overbearing, like a mother would be.

Cody hummed, twisting strands of his dark hair between his fingers. Cody did want to cut it—well, at least make it look presentable, but he rarely had money of his own to do anything, and he wasn't the best at using scissors. His face warmed up thinking about Quinn. The boy never poked fun at his looks or presentation. He knew something stood out about his looks, but Quinn never mentioned it.

He liked that.

He had wanted to walk home with Quinn, but he didn't want to be home today—the next few days even. With one last look at the streets, Cody made his departure. There had to be a nice bench in the park to spend the night.

CHAPTER SEVEN

- -

C ody didn't go to school often, but today he had come in during the third period. He spent the rest of it and the fourth period waiting for lunch, and when it came, he made a beeline to his special spot.

This break was a bit more eventful than most, and Cody soon found himself sitting on the stairs of the back door with a small bird in his hands. He was in the school's backyard that was riddled with weeds, broken furniture, and rocks. He looked up from it from time to time to gaze up to the tree with the nest the bird had fallen from. The mother bird was panicking as she jumped from branch to branch crying from the depth of her belly. Cody wasn't too sure what to do. If he left the bird by the tree it would die because its mother couldn't pick it up, and on the other hand, Cody couldn't climb the tree and return the displaced chick either.

Noise from the school courtyard rang through the entire compound. It was expected during the short thirty-minute break period. Students were playing quick games of soccer or they were catching up with friends from other classes and grades.

Cody looked down at the bird in his hands, farrowing his boys as it watched it gasp for air. It was fifty-percent beak and fifty-percent small pink body covered in soft brown feathers. "What am I supposed to do with you?" he asked in a whisper, leaning forward as he watched its body heave with each breath.

Cody sighed, poking the bird's small body. It quivered, kicking its legs before staying still again.

After a bit, Cody looked over at the tree again. "If only I wasn't just a bag of bones, I would have climbed up to return you." The boy bit his bottom lip in thought, wondering what to do. His eyes went wide as a sudden idea came to him, but he worried that it wouldn't go as planned.

"I should ask Quinn, shouldn't I?" he said out loud, feeling himself shiver at the mere thought of it. Cody knew where Quinn and his friends usually stayed during lunch break, but he was a bit hesitant to walk up to the boy with a small bird in his hand. He worried that Quinn would think his concern for the bird was stupid—or worse, Quinn's friends might pick on him if Quinn pretended not to know him in public. That could happen, even though Quinn had said they were friends. Cody panicked a bit, deciding to abandon the thought.

"Maybe I should try climbing up the tree by myself," Cody said, looking over at the tree again. "No, we'd both die if I tried that. I'd just tumble to the ground with you," he said, shaking his head after giving it another thought. He looked down at the bird in his pal, before rubbing the bird's tiny head with thr tip of a finger.

"I'm going to ask Quinn," he announced to the bird with a small smile.

The skinny boy got up from the concrete stairs before heading out to the main courtyard where most of the school students stayed during the long break.

He looked around the courtyard, his eyes flickering from social group to social group until his eyes landed on the one with Quinn at the center of it. He smiled, taking a deep breath before walking over to Quinn and his group of friends.

When Cody reached them, he hesitated. The taller boys crowded Quinn, and he wasn't sure how to reach out to him. Swallowing his fear, the boy nudged closer.

"Hey." his voice was low, but high enough for the boys' right in front of him to turn and stare. The conversation halted, and soon everyone in the group had their eyes on him.

"I want to talk to Quinn," he managed to get out before his legs could take on a life of their own to run.

"Hey!" Quinn said, moving through the crowd to reach him. Quinn's excited voice made the facial expressions of his friends to relax. They continued talking to each other, while Quinn pulled Cody aside by the arm to talk to him.

"What's up? I think this is the first time I'm seeing you in school," Quinn said. There was a wide smile on his face. He was excited that Cody had come up to him first for one.

Cody remained quiet, making Quinn raise a brown at him.

"Is something wrong?" he asked, reaching out to hold the boy's shoulder.

"Well..." Cody trailed, opening his cupped hands to reveal the bird he had rescued.

"Did it fall from its nest?" Quinn asked, staring down at the baby bird. Cody nodded. He was surprised that Quinn wasn't asking him weird questions, like why he cared so much about a stupid bird. Most people would have told him it was just a bird, the way his brother had told him it was just a cat when Cody cried over the feline his brother had killed by crushing its skull with a baseball bat.

"Can you show me the nest. I'll put it back," Quinn offered, and Cody smiled before nodding. He hadn't even had to ask. Quinn had just taken the initiative. Cody led the way to the nest, and Quinn followed behind him. They were soon at the school backyard. When Cody showed Quinn the nest, Quinn took the bird from him before making his way to the three. He started to climb it, and Cody watched in awe at how easy it was for Quinn to get up and then down.

"There. Its mum pecked my arm, but I'm fine," Quinn said when he got down. He dusting his jeans as a laugh left his lips. His dark hair had a twig in it, but Cody felt it would be rude to reach out to grab it.

Cody smiled. "Thank you."

"Nah, the bird should be thanking you. You kind of saved its life," Quinn insisted. He stared at Cody, mirroring the boy's soft smile before looking away when his face started to warm up. "See you later," he muttered before turning and making his way out of the backyard.

Cody watched as Quinn returned to his friends. He didn't look away until his eyes lost the boy in the crowds. Cody felt a little dazed, and he also felt flustered in an odd way.

It was odd to him—odd to meet a strong charismatic person that didn't look down at him—that didn't use misuse his influence to hurt others.

Cody was frozen in place for a bit. He blinked after staring into space for what seemed like forever. A sigh left his lips as he tucked his hands in his pockets. A little embarrassment came from the little ache that had made a home in his chest. He had briefly—just briefly, thought about Quinn in a way he wasn't supposed to.

He wouldn't want me. Cody thought to himself. Of course, Quinn wouldn't want him. Him with the sickly skin and messy hair. Him that didn't look or act like any of the attractive confident girls that were a much better match for Quinn, so Cody scolded himself and repressed his thoughts, pushing them to the back of his mind where they wouldn't upset the friendship he was building with Quinn.

Quinn would remain a friend.

Because that was the only way Quinn would have him.

CHAPTER EIGHT

The streets were flooded by the orange light of the retreating sun. Quinn and his friends had just finished a game of basketball and were getting ready to head back home together. The boys were grabbing their shoes and socks, and some of them that had hung their t-shirts on the pools were stretching to grab them and put them back on.

Quinn had gotten ready minutes earlier and was losing his patience with his friends. He thought about it for a bit, and after a few minutes of evaluation decided that he had to leave immediately.

"Hey, why are you leaving without us?" Karl asked when he saw Quinn heading towards the gate. "Is something wrong?" he added, raising a brow at his friend who seemed to be ready to jump and sprint.

"I need to go home early," Quinn said, squeezing his hand into a fist and he tightened the grip he had on his school bag handle. "I'll see you guys later," he muttered, heading for the gates without another word before anyone could stop him.

He heard Karl let out a sigh from behind him, and he did hear a few of his other mates' grumble at his decision, but he didn't care. The truth was that he had seen Cody get up a little while ago to leave. He couldn't wait for his friends to grab their stuff. If he did, he would lose Cody before he could catch up to him. It was evening now, and it would get dark soon.

Quinn broke into a run when he walked past the gates. He sprinted through the grass field until he was in the main street maid with concrete and black granite. He looked from end to end before remembering and following the path Cody had taken. He kept running, wondering when he would meet up with the boy. He almost gave up, but when he spotted a dot in the near distance his cheat flooded with relief. Cody was a few meters away. He was wearing jeans today with his usual graphic t-shirt.

"Hey!" Quinn yelled at the top of his lungs when his legs got unbearably tired. He stopped running and crouched over to take deep breaths. "Hey! Cody, please wait!" he yelled, hoping the boy heard him.

To Quinn's relief, the frail boy stopped at the sound of his name. Quinn, stood straight, watching as Cody turned to face Quinn. His eyes went wide with shock, and he cast his gaze to the ground as quickly as he had raised it to look at Quinn. Quinn rose a brow, wondering why the boy looked so blue. He walked up to him, stopping in front of him before touching his shoulder.

"Are you okay?" he asked in a small voice, bending his head so that he could see the side of Cody's face. The boy didn't give him a reply, and that worried Quinn.

"Is something wrong?" Quinn asked, and he was still met with silence. Quinn sighed. "Come on, talk to me," he insisted, taking hold of Cody's face before bringing it up to meet his gaze. Quinn blinked in shock at the sight of the boy. Cody's face and eyes were red and puffy from the silent tears he'd been shedding. There was a bruise forming at the side of his left cheek that was going purple—it wasn't new. It looked about a few hours old.

"W-what happened to you?" Quin asked. His voice was soft, and it shook a bit. He touched the side of Cody's face, careful not to press too hard in order not to cause pain, but Cody flinched anyway, shutting his eyes. It must have really hurt. Quinn's chest squeezed up and a frown took form on his face as anger filled him. He didn't know what to do—where to start. He just knew he wanted to beat the shit out of whoever had touched Cody. It could be people at school, but Quinn was sure he hadn't seen Cody during the break period even though he had searched.

Cody remained silent for a bit, and when he responded his answer wasn't helpful. "N-nothing." He insisted, pushing Quinn's hand away from his face before moving to cover the bruise on his cheek. The boy was heaving, and he refused to make eye contact with Quinn. The two were in the middle of the street, and Quinn was starting to worry that his friends might find them.

"Don't lie to me," Quinn sighed as his expression became worried. "Come on."

Quinn's voice was soft—sweet, and the mere sound of it seemed to send Cody into a fit of sobs. His eyes teared up, and he couldn't keep it in anymore. Quinn stared at the crying boy, unsure of what to do. He eventually took a hold of his shoulder before leading him to the empty stairs of one of the nearby buildings before sitting him down.

Quinn then sat beside the boy before reaching to pulling the small boy's head down with his hand until Cody was resting his head on his shoulder. He didn't ask anything again—he didn't want to hear the throaty cries that sounded like the boy was about to die, so he just stayed quiet and pat Cody's head. After what seemed like hours, the boy stopped shaking from sobs. His silence left a void that was drenched in questions that needed to be asked.

The frail boy heaved before raising his head from Quinn's shoulder. "I'm sorry..." he trailed, wiping his face with the sleeve of his shirt.

Quinn frowned. "For what?"

Cody shrugged. "I don't know. For crying?"

Quinn sighed, reaching to dry under Cody's had with his fingers. "There's nothing to be sorry about." Quinn's words hung in the air like a hook. He waited for Cody to say something. Anything.

"I got into a fight with my brother," the fair boy confessed, looking down at the stairs.

"I see." Were the only words that Quinn could see fit to say. So, he has a brother? He thought to himself. He had never heard of him, but then again Cody had been reluctant to share anything about himself.

Cody felt the bruise on his cheek with his fingers. He winced, pulling them away. "This is why I don't like staying at home. If I get within a foot of him, he'll swing his arms until he hits me."

"What? Why?" Quinn asked as his eyes went wide. He felt that they hadn't gotten along once, but Cody's words meant that this was a recurrent thing.

Cody shrugged. "He doesn't like me, is all. Sibling rivalry and all that bollocks." He laughed, but it was laced with so much anxiety it made Quinn wince.

Quinn sighed, turning to look at Cody with a frown. "You expect me to believe that?"

Cody brought his thumb finger to his lips. "No, not really," he muttered, chewing the nail.

Quinn felt frustrated. "He's bullying you—"

"Everyone bullies me. It's not new," Cody said, cutting Quinn off before he could finish his sentence. "It's just how it is," he added. His nihilism cloaked Quinn with dread. The whole thing was depressing. Cody was being depressing.

"Do your parents know?" Quinn asked, saying something so that the weight of the silence wouldn't crush him under its weight.

Cody sighed. "Yeah, my mum knows, and she really doesn't care. He'll probably hit her too if she said anything."

Quinn sighed, not knowing what to say to that. Dysfunctional families were common in the town. Poor finances meant frustrated adults, and frustrated adults meant poor coping mechanisms like drugs, violence, and alcohol. The kids and teens in town just seemed to learn how to work around it. Cody's case wasn't special in the least.

"You don't have to stay here with me you know?" Cody said in a soft voice, breaking the silence. "You can leave. It's getting dark." He added, rubbing his eyes with the back of his hand.

"What about you? You're not going home, are you?" Quinn asked, and Cody froze up, refusing to meet Quinn's gaze.

A sigh left Quinn's lips. "You can come to stay at my place for a bit, then maybe you can sneak back into your place early in the morning. Does that sound good?" Quinn asked, watching Cody's expression shift, but the boy remained silent.

Quinn leaned forward so that he could look at Cody's face properly. "Is that a yes or a no?"

"It's a yes." Cody's words came out in a croak, but Quinn heard him. "That would be nice if your parents don't mind," Cody added and Quinn gave him a soft smile.

"They won't," Quinn muttered, reaching out to squeeze Cody's knee. His face warmed up when he had noticed what he had done.

Quinn took his hand away. "I hope you're not a picky eater," he muttered, after a while of trying to remember what was in the fridge but not coming up with anything.

"Anything's fine," Cody muttered, hugging his knees. His face was burning from Quinn's action from before. He wondered what was wrong with the taller boy. Did he just like touching people for no reason?

"Great!" Quinn grinned before getting up and reaching out his hand to Cody. Cody took it, and Quinn helped him get up from the step as well.

"We'll have to do something about your wounds first," Quinn said, reaching to touch Cody's cheek again. "We should have a bag of peas in the freezer," he said before taking his hand away.

"We'll get the swelling down, and I can warm up something for you to eat," Quinn said. "We'll have to share my bed, or I could lay down a mat for you on the floor," Quinn went on as the two climbed down the stairs.

Cody nodded. "Okay," he muttered, letting Quinn lead the way. Their hands remained entwined throughout their walk. Sometimes Quinn would squeeze Cody's hand, and the boy's hand and the boy would feel his body warm-up with delight. Quinn's hand was bigger, though softer than his rough ones. It felt nice to hold. He wanted to hold it forever.

CHAPTER NINE

In Quinn's home, the space for the dining room, kitchen, and living room were the same and only separated by diffraction in flooring. The room was lit in orange fluorescence light that reflected off the old worn-out furniture and titled kitchenette floors. Quinn was sitting next to Cody on the sofa. The two boys were sipping soup with metal spoons from the small bowls they held in their hands.

"How is it?" Quinn asked, looking over at Cody who had just put a spoonful of soup in his mouth.

"Good," Cody muttered after swallowing. "It's really nice," he added, as his eyes flickered to Quinn for a bit.

Quinn smiled. "That's good to hear, my mum's good at cooking." He pulled his legs up on the couch, watching as Cody mirrored his smile. The two boys stared at each other, but their gazes were soon stolen by the window when lightning flashed, and thunder followed. It had started drizzling when they had first gotten to the apartment, but now it was a full-on storm.

"Huh, it's getting really bad..." Quinn trailed, wondering if his sister and mum would elect to sleepover at work today.

The drops of rain hitting the window made a tricking sound that got louder with time. Quinn got up then, going to grab a bowl to place under the area of the roof that leaked during storms. He headed back to the Sofa when he was done, before looking over at Cody who still had a bowl in his hands.

"Are you done?" Quinn asked, gesturing to the bowl. "I could put it away for you if you are."

"I am," Cody said, getting up.

Quinn reached out to pull at his shirt. "I said I would put it away for you, didn't I?" He smiled at the boy who gave him the bowl after hesitating for a bit. Cody sat back down, watching Quinn head over to the sink to wash both their bowls. The taller boy returned to the sofa soon after, and he sat closer to Cody than he had initially done.

"Rain sucks, doesn't it?" Quinn muttered, trying to start a conversation.

Cody chuckled. "I guess." He shrugged, pulling his legs up to hug them to himself. His feet were naked now, and Quinn could see the series of scars on them. He wondered if those had anything to do with the boy's brother.

Quinn hummed. "Everything gets all wet and sticky. My sneakers aren't going to like the mud tomorrow."

A laugh escaped Cody's lips. "But it's sort of like natural air conditioning, isn't it?" he said, staring at Quinn.

Quinn's brows farrow as he things about it "Yeah, I guess sort, but can't it be cold without you know—messing up the place?"

Cody laughed at that, and a silence swallowed the room when he stopped. The boy cocked his head at Quinn. He noticed how tired the taller boy looked under the dim lights. His brown eyes were dull, and the smile he had on barely reached his eyes.

"Are you tired?" Cody asked, reaching to touch Quinn's arm.

"Yeah, a little bit," Quinn yawned, rubbing his eyes.

Cody thought for a bit. "Maybe I should leave so you can sleep?" he offered.

"It's okay, I still have to stay up and wait for my parents to come back. I know my sister is at her friend's place if she finished her shift early, but my parents don't usually come back till ten," Quinn said. "Also, you said that you'd stay over."

"I know," Cody said, still feeling a bit self-conscious about Quinn's offer. "That's late," he said, referring to Quinn's sentence about his parents not coming home in a bit.

"Yeah, they do overtime a lot. I wish I could work a bit, but they don't want me to yet. Ah, they're that kind of parents who like to put the full burden on themselves," Quinn said.

"I just wish they live long enough for me and my sister to pay them back," Quinn muttered under his breath. He knew that they didn't have the best life, but his parents put a lot to make sure the walls of their future didn't crumble around them. So many families were dysfunctional, and many teens had already been hard cracked for their future.

"Oh," Cody sighed. The living room fell into an awkward silence, and the sound of the fan turning above was the only thing to tint it. The sound of the fan's blades spinning and the sound of the drops of water hitting the metal bowl from the area of the roof that leaked resounded through the small apartment. QUINN eventually put the TV on, getting up to look through some CDs before selecting one to play.

"We should watch something if I plan to stay up," Quinn said when he sunk down on the sofa again.

"Yeah, I guess so," Cody muttered, cuddling his legs before staring out into the lights coming from the television. The little living room only had a sofa and one single sitter pressed against a storage shelf of DVDs. The window didn't have any curtains, and the floor would be bare if the apartment hadn't come with its own carpets.

The movie Quinn had put was an old horror film with awful film effects, and Quinn and Cody spent most of the night laughing instead of screaming in horror.

They both turned towards the main door when it creaked open, watching as Quinn's mother, a brown-skinned woman who looked to be in her early forties walked in. She was in plain blue jeans and a cream top, and it didn't take long for a man around the same age range to walk in after her.

"Quinn, is that Karl?" Quinn's mother asked as she took off her shoes and dropped her bag on the kitchen counter. The lady had afro-textured hair and full lips, and the man that had followed behind her looked more like Quinn with his wavy hair and light brown skin.

"No this is Cody, he's staying over this night," Quinn said.

Quinn's mother nodded. "Okay, did you at least feed him?" she asked as she started to take out groceries and put them away.

Quinn smiled. "Yes, ma'am." Quin rolled his eyes at his dad who hadn't said anything yet. "He likes your cooking, mum."

Quinn's father opened a can of beer. "Everyone loves your mum's cooking."

Quinn chuckled at that, getting up to go help his mother put things away.

Cody watched Quinn and his parents interact. It was fascinating to him, to say the least. He'd learned to be wary of adults—flying hands and screaming were always a possibility. Cody continued to watch in awe. Quinn's father ruffled his hair, and Quinn's mum gave him a hug when they put everything away. The two adults soon disappeared into the hallway as they headed for their bedroom. Quinn turned off the television, before giving Cody a smile.

"Let's go to my room," he said, making the smaller boy get up. Cody followed Quinn through the hallway and walked into the small room Quinn lead him into. He looked around the tiny space when Quinn abandoned him to open the windows. Cool after-storm area drifted in as Quinn hummed.

Cody didn't know what to do, so he stood by the door while holding on to his arm as he stared at Quinn's posters—they were mostly of comic heroes, but some of them were from the bands they had talked about when they first interacted properly.

"Here," Quinn said, stealing the boy's attention from the posters. "You can wear this," he added, walking over to hand Cody a pair of shorts and a shirt to change into.

Cody thanked him, turning around to take of his items of clothes one at a time before changing. He was glad to have fresh clothes, but now he wasn't sure where he was going to sleep. There was only one bed, and Quinn had already gone to lie on it.

Quinn looked over at Cody, wondering why he hadn't hopped into bed. He tapped the area beside him, shifting a little to create more space. "Come on, it's cold."

Cody didn't move. The boy just stared on with wide eyes as his chest squeezed up.

Quinn, being worried, sat up. "Is something wrong?"

The boy shook his head. "No," he said as he walked over to the bed before climbing in. The lay down in silence for a while, both of them listening to the other's breathing as a thing neither of them wanted to address loomed above them.

"It's not gay if that's what you're worried about." Quinn's words were riddled with anxiety, and the laugh he tried to mask it in didn't work.

Cody didn't laugh. He felt like his heart was in his throat. He couldn't really explain the feeling—it felt like he was sick—frustrated, panicked, distressed. Was the feeling restlessness?

Since Cody didn't answer him Quinn turned to face the wall. The rustling in bed made Cody turn to. He stared on at Quinn's back, watching as his side rose and fell with his breathing. It was dark, but Quinn had left one of the orange fluorescence lights on. It drowned the room in a light yellow-orange, and it made Quinn's dark hair look brown. Cody wanted to touch his hair. Cody wanted to reach out and touch the boy's waist.

He swallowed the spit building up at the back of his mouth. Maybe I can wish it away. Cody thought as a sigh escaped his lips.

He knew wishing his feelings away wouldn't work, but he decided he would try. Through the night he tried his best to sleep, but he was restless for most of it. He only shut his eyes when the deep dark blue darkness turned to a tinted morning grey. He drifted off to sleep in the early hours of dawn, one of his hands still managing to touch Quinn's back in a reach for comfort—warmth.

CHAPTER TEN

- -

T he school's cafeteria was a medium-sized hall with wooden tables that could take up to eight students at a time. Usually, Quinn would sit with his friends on the table closest to the door, but today Quinn was on a table at the back sitting next to Cody whose usual pale colorful face was red. Having slept over meant that Cody stuck around when Quinn got ready for school and tagged along with the boy.

Cody looked stressed. And his eyes were fixated on the plate in front of him as his hands gripped at the cloth of his jeans. He rarely ever visited the cafeteria—he rarely ever went to school at all, so it was strange to be in the sea of students as the smell of food hung in the air. Worst still, people couldn't take their eyes off both of them. Cody wondered if Quinn saw what he saw.

"Are you worried about something?" Quinn asked, cocking his head a bit so that he could look at Cody's face properly.

"N-no, I'm n-not..." Cody trailed, looking up from his plate of beans. His voice was shaky, and the way he twitched when Quinn leaned forward with a frown discounted his words.

"You look uncomfortable," Quinn stated, and Cody shrugged his shoulders.

The fair boy sighed. "People are staring at us," he said, picking up the plastic fork in his tray to poke at the beans.

The crease of Quinn's frown deepened at Cody's words. He looked up, noticing what Cody had said. The whole cafeteria was indeed looking their way. Some people turned away when Quinn turned his gaze to them, but Karl and Lindsey had their eyes still fixed on him and Cody. The confusion was clear on everyone's face. Most people wondered what Quinn was doing with the weird kid that moved around the school building like a ghost. Quinn was known for being barely two meters away from his friend group, and now he was sitting with a kid who was—in kind words—the school's outcast.

Karl turned when Quinn rose a brow at him, but Lindsey continued to stare before she made to whisper into a friend's ear.

"I don't feel very well," Cody admitted. "I don't like being watched." Cody didn't have much time left in school, so he preferred to remain unknown. Having people up in his business was not something he wanted at all.

"Do you want me to leave?" Quinn asked after a while of being silent. There was a sadness in his tone. He didn't want to leave, but if it made Cody uncomfortable he would leave. Cody found himself staring down at his food as he tried to think up an answer to Quinn's proposal. He wanted the staring to stop, but he didn't want Quinn to leave.

"Do what you want," he ended up says before shrugging his shoulders. When Quinn had spotted him the cafeteria and left his friends to join him, Cody had been a bit surprised. Quinn had walked over to him with a smile and offered him food he has watched his mother pack for him as they had left his house together that morning.

Quinn sighed, frustrated. "You should really start saying more of yes or no."

Cody froze up at Quinn's voice, scared that the boy might be angry at him. He looked up, and visibly sighed in relief when he noticed Quinn was smiling at him. "I really don't know. You can leave if you want. I don't want people to give you trouble because of me—"

"I'll stay," Quinn said, cutting Cody off. There were about thirty minutes left for lunch, and Quinn wasn't going to leave the boy alone by himself. Cody was hard to catch in and out of school, and Quinn realized that they might not get to talk to each other for a while if he left now.

Cody blinked, before focusing his gaze on the wooden table. "Okay." The decision Quinn made brought him joy, but he wasn't going to express that to him. Instead, he tried to hide his grin by stuffing more food in his mouth.

Although the cafeteria stared on, Quinn stayed with Cody, easing his anxiousness by talking to the smaller boy. Quinn started a discussion about birds that made the frail boy a fast talker with little breath between his words. Quinn was amused by his excitement.

"You've forgotten about all the staring," Quinn said, and Cody froze up again, looking about the cafeteria before recoiling into himself again.

I shouldn't have said that. Quinn thought, scolding himself. He found it a bit perplexing that Cody seemed so scared. The other kids were just looking because they were curious. It wasn't a death sentence—Quinn would know, he got stared at all the time.

"You can pretend they're all little jaybirds, you know?" Quinn said, and Cody chuckled, looking up again. The talked about jaybirds, and Quinn smiled when he noticed that Cody seemed at ease again. The conversation soon veered towards the comic book Quinn had both for him way back.

"Did you like it?"

"Yeah," Cody said, taking a sip of water from the open bottle on his tray.

There was a pause.

"Did you sneak in just fine?" Quinn asked, starting up another conversation. When they had both left his place, Quinn had to wait for about thirty minutes at a crossroad for Cody to get his stuff from home.

Cody frowned for a bit, swallowing the food in his mouth before his features relaxed when he realized what Quinn must be talking about. "Yeah, I did. I didn't see my brother either."

"That's good to hear," Quinn muttered, resting his head on his raised hands. He had finished his food a while back. His eyes glanced at Cody's plate. It was still half full. Something he had noticed was that the boy was slow with meals. It seemed like he was overwhelmed by them—like he didn't eat much and wasn't used to it.

A smile touched Cody's lips. "Thanks for letting me stay over at your place."

"It's no problem. It was nice to have company as I waited for my parents," Quinn muttered, resting his head on the cool wooden surface of the table as he smiled up at Cody.

"Are your parents always that nice?" Cody asked in a small voice as Quinn closed his eyes and hummed.

"Yes, they're always like that."

I'm jealous. Cody wanted to say, but he didn't want to stir the conversation in an uncomfortable direction. Besides, he didn't want to rant about his mum and brother now. Quinn was being nice to him, but that would be a lot to drop on the boy for no reason.

"Your mum's very good at cooking," Cody said instead, scooping a spoon full of beans.

Quinn chuckled. "Yeah, she is." He drummed a finger on the table, feeling bored. "When you came over you looked at my posters a lot. Do you want any of my records? I have lots of them to share," Quinn said, mentioning the band posters he had up. Cody felt his face warm up. A big part of why he had stared at the walls was because he didn't want to stare at Quinn changing. He had got a glimpse though. His chest was toned, and he had nice legs under the jogging pants he wore every day.

"I like A Dozen Newts, but do you think it's okay if you gave me your stuff like that?" Cody asked, chewing inside his mouth. "I'm wearing your clothes now that I think about it," he added, realizing that Quinn had given him the nice graphic tee and trousers he had on. They were a little too big for him because Quinn was taller and broader, but they were alright.

"Friends share things," Quinn said after a while. "So yeah, it's okay," Quinn said and Cody's face warmed up at that.

The two continued to talk about mundane things. Homework, comic books, and bands. Their discussion was interrupted by a chough that made them both turn their gaze up. Quinn frowned when he realized it was Lindsey. She had an odd smile on her face and was wearing faded blue jeans that she matched with a denim top.

"What do you want?" Quinn asked when she didn't say anything after a while. She cocked her head to the side, making her braids fall in that direction as well. She was squinting at them both.

The girl shrugged, folding her hands over her chest as her eyes flickered form Quinn to Cody. "Nothing, I just came to take a closer look."

Cody, feeling uncomfortable looked away from her to stare at Quinn. Cody began to wonder if he was now in the middle of a lover's quarrel.

Quinn never told him if he said yes or no to Lindsey asking him out. He looked over at her, wondering if she was the person Quinn was dating. He had seemed worried when they had talked about it at the basketball court, but maybe the two had sorted things out. Cody thought Quinn had to be dating someone, girls were always flocking about him, so it only made sense.

Lindsey was also very pretty.

She was 5'0 feet of manic pixie dream girl. That's what the girls were into these days—or at least that's the impression, Cody.

Quinn let out a sigh before looking down at his plate. "Well then, have a long hard look." Cody frowned, wondering if there was something he didn't know.

After a while, Lindsey did leave, but she didn't go without making a blowing motion with her hands as she sucked on her cheeks. Quinn didn't seem to notice, but Cody felt like a bucket of cold water had been poured on him.

Does she know I like him? Cody thought to himself, making his hands into fists in attempts to stop them from shaking. The possibility made him nervous. He didn't know what would happen if Quinn knew. He didn't want to let go of his new friend.

PART TWO | MY HEART BEATS FOR YOU

P ART TWO

MY HEART BEATS FOR YOU

"One is loved because one is loved. No reason is needed for loving." ——
Paulo Coelho

CHAPTER ELEVEN

The sitting room/kitchen of Quinn's family's apartment was quiet today. It was late on a Sunday afternoon, and Quinn's sister—Janet—was reading a book on the couch as Quinn watched her from behind the kitchen counter. Janet was a few years older than Quinn—twenty. She had started working straight out of high school, and now helped maintain a hair salon.

Quinn wondered about, sighing and huffing, hoping he would catch his sister's attention. The girl ignored him, licking her finger before flipping to another page of her book. The two weren't very close but Quinn often went to his sister for advice like he was trying to do now.

Frustrated, Quinn decided to let it out. "I like him," he said, watching his sister, to see if she would react to his out of place words.

Janet shrugged. "You like who you like," she said, flipping to the next page of the book in her hands. A romance novel. Janet and Quinn's mother were big fans of the cheap second-hand books they got from the gas station convenience store.

Quinn sighed before looking up at the ceiling patched with wet stains. It had been raining frequently, and their roof didn't look like it was taking it well. It was odd how the rainwater trickled down through the cracks and through all floors.

Quinn looked down at his fingers, letting out a groan "I guess I like who I like, sure, but what should I do about it? Should I just keep quiet about it or—"

"Whatever you want to do. Why are you asking me even?" Janet asked, looking up from her book before giving her little brother a frown. She had dark skin and loose full curls that ended at the nape of her neck.

Quinn laughed, understanding his sister's frustration with him. He knew he was being whiny, but he wanted proper advice from her, not her 'leave me alone' one-liners.

Janet sighed when Quinn didn't say anything in response. She cocked her head to the side, making her brown curls fall to the side with her action.

"Though, if I were you, I would tell him. I'm not sure if you notice the way he looks at you. It's quite endearing," Janet said, watching her brother's face grow warm with her words.

Quinn looked up from his fingers to stare at his sister. "Really?" He could hear his heart beating his ears. He hadn't really noticed anything. In fact, he'd thought maybe Cody was bored of hanging out with him. Cody had come to his place a few more times when he couldn't go home, and he'd met Quinn's sister once.

"Yup, but it could be a savior complex thing, you do kind of protect him. I don't know... I might be reading into things too much." Janet watched her brother sigh.

That was true. Quinn gave Cody a lot of things. Food, clothes, and protection at school. Of course, Quinn was doing all that because he wanted to help. He also liked Cody there was that, but he didn't want things to go in a transactional way. Throwing gifts at someone until they liked you wasn't the way to go about things.

Quinn ran his fingers through his hair before nibbling on his lips as he thought of what to do. He'd recently come to terms with the fact that his feelings were more complicated than being a crush. His thoughts might have been easy to ignore when they were just isolated thoughts like 'His eyes are beautiful', and 'He's cute', but realization crashed down on him when Cody started clouding his thoughts in more intimate ways. He'd get worried about it. He wanted to be around him, and it'd crossed the line when he realized Cody was all he wanted to think about when he tried to masturbate like any normal teenage male.

Quinn's face starts to heat up. "So, do I just say I like you? That's kind of all out there, and direct—"

"Look, I really don't know. Maybe ask him on a date?" Janet said, cutting her brother off before closing her book and putting it aside.

"Oh..." Was all Quinn could muster as he ran a hand through his head of hair.

"I'm not sure why you like him, though. He seemed like a bit of an airhead, but he's cute, I guess. A little messy looking, but cute," Janet said, smiling when she caught bother's eyes when they flickered to her. They both had deep brown eyes.

The boy groaned, rolling his eyes at his sister.

Janet could poke fun at Quinn all she wanted, but she didn't really know Cody—Quinn knew Cody. There was just something pure and delicate about him that Quinn liked. Cody, the boy that helped animals and picked his words carefully not to cause offense. The boy who enjoyed talking about comics and games you could find in newspapers.

It's been a few weeks, and Quinn and Cody had just grown closer. He still talked to his group of friends, but he found every excuse to spend that time with Cody.

"Why do you hang out with him so much?" Hozier had asked him once as they emptied their lockers for the day at school. Quinn had just grinned at him, sidestepping before wandering off to find Cody who hid in the school bathrooms or took a nap in the backyard that was an injury hazard fest.

"He's not an airhead, just a bit quiet," Quinn said, coming out of his thoughts. A smile formed on his lips as a memory of him and Cody sharing chips from the same bag as they walked back home together filled his mind.

Janet shrugged. "He seemed afraid when I met him. He was acting like I would pounce on him or something, and I'm tiny and terrible at fighting so that's not even possible." She laughed, showing the cute gap in her teeth.

Silence followed since Quinn didn't reply to his sister's words. He decided that it was better not to air Cody's personal business, even though he had the urge to explain why he was like that.

"I'm going to my room," Quinn announced walking towards the door that led to the hallway.

Janet nodded, picking up her book again before flipping to the page she had stopped at. "Don't oversleep. If you're not up for dinner you won't have it at all."

"Noted," Quinn said, slipping into the hallway before heading for his room.

Quinn threw himself on the mattress of his bed when he got to his room. He closed his eyes, burying his face on the pillow Cody had used when he slept over on Thursday. He missed the boy. They hadn't seen each other since the weekend and Cody didn't have a phone, so it wasn't like Quinn could call him. Quinn had wanted to ask him if he was free on the weekend when they parted ways on Friday, but he chickened out. Convinced that would be pushing too hard.

He rolled on his bed, pulling out his phone from his back pocket before looking up the page he had googled the other day in his bookmarks. He had tried bringing up the topic of sex with his friends the other day, and they had looked at him in horror before going into graphic detail about sleeping with girls. The boys talked about it often enough, but there was special attention put into talking to him. It was the first time Quinn had brought up the topic himself.

"They like it when you lick their chest," one of the boys in his friend group had said while pretending to be buried between boobs. "Like this."

The whole thing had made Quinn cringe. That hadn't been what he had wanted. He had wanted advice on how to do it with a boy—but he didn't ask directly, and they talked to him about girls instead.

"Check online if you want to learn how to do it that way," Karl had whispered to him as they went to their last class that day. He had turned to him, looking at his friend with wide eyes.

"I know what's happening," the brown-haired boys had said. "I don't see you any differently," was all he had mouthed before tapping Quinn's shoulder and wandering to his seat at the back.

After that Quinn had spent a lot of time thinking. He knew they were in a small town, and he knew not everyone was the most open-minded. He spent his walk home thinking about the issues that came with liking Coby. People might bully them—Quinn crossed that out because he would just hit them. Their parents might not approve. Quinn knew his sister wouldn't care, but it would be weird talking to his catholic parents about it. He swallowed the spit in the back of his mouth and closed his eyes shut before opening them again.

He decided that it wouldn't kill him to tell his parents when he and Cody started dating.

If.

He was getting ahead of himself. He knew that, but he decided that there wasn't any harm in wishing the future into existence. Somehow, he would get Cody to like him back.

Somehow.

Quinn did what Kyle had told him to when he got home that day, and ever since Quinn would spend a few minutes every night looking through things. A frown formed on Quinn's face. So many words, so many terms, so many orientations, and precautions—his brain hurt. He just wanted to know how to approach Cody properly, and maybe how to go about things if they ever got to be that intimate with each other.

His face flushed when his mind drifted to that time Cody had shown him a mole on his stomach. Cute mole, but not as cute as his belly button. As Quinn's face grew warmer, he curled up to a ball, burying his phone under his pillow as he took in deep breaths.

Big doe eyes, slender limbs—the pinkest of lips.

He wanted to kiss the boy.

He nibbled on the nail of his thumb, closing his eyes before imagining just that.

How would Cody's lips feel? Something told Quinn that they'd taste like the sweets he liked to eat.

CHAPTER TWELVE

Quinn was a little distance away from the basketball court. His friends had left him after their game, allowing him to meet Cody who had been sitting on the stairway from view. It was about six in the evening, and the two boys decided to walk home together.

"You look tired," Quinn said when he turned to look at Cody. He reached out to pat the boy's hair, before taking his hand away. Cody was wearing a green flannel over a graphic t-shirt today. His jean trousers hiked up around his ankles—old and too small for him, but at least his get-up was something different. He had grown self-conscious of the fact that he wore more or less the same thing every day around Quinn. His hair wasn't cut, but it was properly combed. It had all been worth it because Quinn had complimented him in the hallway just before the first period.

A smile formed on Cody's lips when he remembered that. "Yeah, I'm a bit tired," he said, answering Quinn's question before yawning a bit. Their walk continued in silence. The streets were quiet, most kids had already gotten home since classes ended a bit early today. The silence wasn't uncomfortable, but Quinn was tense because he had something to say to Cody before they parted ways today. Every step was a reminder that they were getting closer to where Cody would have to drop off. Quinn turned to look over at Cody from time to time, or he would look at him from the side of his eyes if he felt he'd exceeded the number of glances per minute that wasn't questionable. He noticed that Cody looked better than he usually did. A bruise he had gotten a week ago from his brother had faded, and his skin looked a lot more healthy—tinted and glowing.

At a point, Cody turned, and the boys' eyes met. Quinn felt his face warm up his face, so he looked away before Cody could say anything. The two continued to walk together in the direction of Cody's home. The street the boy lived in was a few blocks before the street Quinn's apartment was in. It was in a worse side of town with cheap bungalows and trailer homes. The silence between them as they walked was filled with the sound of birds, their treading feet and the occasional car that passed by.

It was comfortable, so neither of them bothered to speak, but the silence didn't last, and was interrupted by a squeaking rat tumbling out of an aluminum trashcan that tipped over and rolled on the floor. Cody let out a squeak, jumping at the sight of the rat making a run for it. Quinn laughed, taking hold of Cody's hand before he could run in the other direction.

"It's just a rat. It's afraid of you. Clam down," Quinn said, but Cody didn't look convinced. The boy pulled his hand away from Quinn's grip before making to hug himself as his eyes shut close.

"No. I don't care," Cody said, as his eyes darted to the tipped bin, expecting something else to run out of it. Quinn laughed at him, amused that there was an animal the boy was afraid of. Since he and Cody started walking home together, the boy would be the first to approach stray dogs and cats, but apparently rats weren't in the strays to approach list. The two boys stood by the capsized bin, and Cody stared at it for a while before deciding nothing else was going to zoom out. He let out a sigh, taking his hands off his shoulders as he relaxed.

Cody laughed, smiling a bit. "I feel embarrassed for squeaking now," he said.

Quinn looked at him from the side of his eyes, remembering the cute sound that had escaped the boy's lips. "It's okay, it was cute." The words slipped out on their own before Quinn could catch them. His eyes went wide, and so did Cody's who was now looking at him with bright red cheeks. Cody opened his mouth like he wanted to say something before turning away sharply.

Cody hoped that Quinn didn't catch his redness. His face was burning, and he had no doubt that he looked like a tomato. The two boys continued walking. It was late in the evening now, so the streetlights were on. From time to time Cody would look over at Quinn. He still hadn't gotten over Quinn calling him cute. He wondered if all the little compliments Quinn gave him were intentional—and that if they were what were they for? Were they to tease him, or genuinely compliment him?

The sound of their feet on the sidewalk was starting to annoy Quinn. It was odd for Cody not to say anything on their walks. He looked over at the boy, wondering if he had gone a little too far back there. He raised a brow at the boy, noticing how panicky he seemed. His hands would grasp and leave the straps of his backpack at intervals. The boy suddenly stopped, taking in a deep breath as he stared at the sidewalk with wide eyes.

"What's wrong?" Quinn asked, stopping in his tracks too. Cody blinked, realizing that he had stopped walking.

"Nothing," Cody claimed, shaking his head. His longish dark hair bobbed about with the action before settling down. There was no way he was going to tell Quinn about how he was feeling. There was no way he was going to tell him about how his chest was squeezing up as his heart fluttered. Quinn such an effect on him, and he was starting to wonder if he would be able to control himself around him in the future.

Quinn rose a brow, walking again when Cody started moving forward. He trailed behind him, noticing how stiff his shoulders were. "Are you sure?" he asked in a soft voice, just high enough to pick up.

"Y-yeah." Cody managed. His heart was beating fast, and he felt so warm—like he had a fever.

Quinn let out a sigh, looking away from the boy. He didn't say anything since Cody didn't look like he was in the mood to talk. It would be awful if he had made Cody uncomfortable with his words. He cursed his dumb thoughts for finding their way out of his mouth.

They soon got to Cody's house. It was a small flat at the beginning of one of the roads. The lights were off, and Quinn could hear Cody let out an audible groan. Cody really didn't like going home when his family members were awake. Quinn wanted to suggest that he just sleepover at his place, but Cody had been doing that a lot, and at a point, he figured it was weird to ask him to sleep in his bed so regularly.

The two boys stood still, both staring at the house in front of them until Cody sighed. The boy squared his shoulders, tightening his grip on his backpack before willing himself to head home. "See you then—" He got distracted and couldn't finish his sentence because Quinn had taken a hold of his hand. Cody staggered back, turning to face Quinn who was looking at him with wide eyes.

"Wait..." Quinn muttered, letting go of Cody's hand. "I have something to tell you," he said, biting down on his lower lip as he stared down at the grass.

"What is it?" Cody asked, cocking his head to the side ad a small frown played on his face. He wondered what could have Quinn so nervous.

Quinn opens his mouth, but nothing comes out. He sighs, looking up at Cody. Cody wondered what was so hard for Quinn to blurt out. His breathing hiked up and his heart began to beat faster when he realized that maybe Quinn didn't want to be friends with him anymore. He knew it. Their friendship was too good to be true—

"Do you want to go out sometime, like downtown to eat or watch a movie?" Quinn asked, cutting off Cody's train of thought. "Like a date..." he added, feeling his face warm up again, so he looked down at the grass.

Cody blinked. "What?" The boy wondered if he'd heard Quinn right.

Quinn could feel the confidence drain out of his pores, but he wasn't backing down now.

"Do you want to go on a date with me?" Quinn repeated, proud of the fact that he had managed to keep his voice clear instead of melting into a blubbering mess.

Cody looked down at his tennis shoes, not sure of how to reply. His body was bursting with joy, and his head had gone numb from equally shock and delight.

Quinn started to panic again. "You can say no. I just like you a lot, and I thought I'd ask you instead of keeping quiet about it—"

"Okay," Cody replied, cutting Quinn off. He wasn't going to let him take it back.

Quinn's eyes went wide before a grin broke across his lips. "You won't regret saying yes, I promise. I'll tell you where we're going tomorrow. Does that sound okay?"

"Yeah," Cody said, smiling. "It does."

The two boys looked at each other in the dimly lit street, both red-faced and nervous. It was like they expected the other to do something—make a move. None of them wanting to pathways.

"I-I should be going," Cody said, breaking up the staring fest.

"Yeah, me too," Quinn said after a chuckle. "See you tomorrow."

Cody smiled at him, turning away before walking in direction of his front door. Quinn watched the small boy as he opened the door and walked into his house. He waited by the pavement for a while before turning away and heading back home. The smile on his face hadn't disappeared, and his sister poked fun at him for it when he got home but he didn't care. Cody had said yes to going on a date with him. That was all that mattered.

CHAPTER THIRTEEN

W hen Cody had walked into the house, he had expected his brother to be either passed out on the sofa or ready to knock his teeth out for whatever reason he could come up with that night. Instead, Cody found a lit mudroom, and an empty kitchen/living room area. He took off his shoes and searched the fridge for something to eat. He stood at the kitchen counter, gobbling up the bowl of cereal and his head turned towards the hallway drowned in yellow light from time to time to make sure his brother couldn't catch him eating. When he was done eating, he washed the bowl and put it away, becoming confident that his mother and brother were indeed fast asleep.

The small living room in Cody's bungalow home was covered with a cheap carpet to hide the cracks on the tiles below. The television was placed on the floor since there wasn't any table it could sit on. There was a pile of scattered CD cases next to it. The flashing lights from the screen pierced Cody's eyes in the dark. The lights were off, but the boy was on the sofa, flipping through T.V. channels before settling on a low budget soap opera that was playing. As much as Cody despised his brother, he did pay for the television bill, and the rent, and the water—and everything. It was one of the reasons he remained meek around him. He still needed a place to live and food to eat.

The room was cool since the night was windy and cool breeze filtered in through the netted windows. As Cody watched the drama show, a smile formed on his face as he remembered his interaction with Quinn. how flustered the both of them had been as Quinn had worked up the courage to ask him that question.

Cody was still shocked.

Quinn had asked him out and it hadn't been a dream.

Cody's face heated up as he thought of all the times Quinn would do something out of place, and he would hope it was something more before beating the mere thought of the possibility out of his mind. His wishful thinking had been on to something, and now he could stop panicking about his crush on Quinn and ease into it.

I wonder... He thought to himself, watching as the couple in the television share a kiss. He swallowed back the spit that formed in the back of his mouth at the thought of it. If Quinn liked him that way too, that meant that the boy wanted to kiss him, right? He raised his fingers to his face, feeling his lips with the tips of his fingers as his mind dared to imagine it. He curled up on the sofa, guessing that Quinn's full lips would be soft on his—warm when applying pressure.

He shut his eyes, trying to calm down before he got too excited. Cody had known he was gay for a long time. It hadn't been something that had jumped out of nowhere, but it had been a gradual realization over time. His life hadn't just been stable enough for him to act out on his hormones like other teens. While people fuzzed about dating, Cody worried about stepping into his own house or meeting up with his brother. He hadn't seen Quinn in that way at first, but over time he couldn't ignore the pilling feeling of longing tangled up with gratitude when he spent time with Quinn.

He let out a sigh, smiling against his fingers before putting them away. It wasn't something he should worry about. Quinn was always quick to leave him alone when he didn't want to do anything, and Quinn was always vocal when he wanted to do or share anything with Cody. The boy assumed it would be the same with everything else—including physical intimacy.

There was nothing to worry about.

"What are you smiling about, brat?" Cody felt his blood run cold at the sound of his brother's voice. He had assumed everyone had gone to bed, but apparently not.

Cody turned to look at his brother who was standing by the entrance to the hallway. "Nothing," Cody said, answering his question from before as his eyes moved to stare down at the black carpet. "I'm not smiling at anything, Charles."

Charles ignores his answer, deciding to yell at him instead. "What the fuck are you smiling for? You think you have the right to be happy, don't you? Well, you don't."

Cody swallowed the saliva that built up at the back of his throat. He could feel himself shaking, but he kept his composure by staring at the carpet and not raising his gaze to meet Charles.

"You're not going to say anything?" Charles asked, and Cody remained quiet as the drama show on television filled the void with its dramatic sound and cue effects.

Cody heard footsteps come his way, and he started to panic. He could sense Charles was hovering over him, standing right behind the sofa he was sitting on.

"You were smiling just a minute ago," Charles said, not wanting to let it go. He laughed, knocking Cody's head. "What's wrong? Cat's got your tongue?"

Cody refused to answer, keeping his eyes on the ground as his brother continued to harass him. He was used to it, and if he was lucky, he would get out with just a slap in the face and nothing more. Cody could smell the alcohol on his brother's clothes. It was nauseating.

Cody let out a gasp when he was pushed forward by the head. He tumbles off the couch, kneeling over on the floor. He gritted his teeth and shut his eyes tight, but he didn't say anything.

"You're still not going to talk?" Charles' voice was right in front of him now. The older boy must have moved closer to continue harassing him.

Cody, against his better judgment, spoke up. "What do you want me to say?" he asked, opening his eyes before rubbing at the part of his head Cody had soccer punched. "What?" Cody asked again, looking up at his brother with a fed-up look in his eyes.

Charles frowns down at him. "What were you smiling about?"

Cody sighed. "I came back from watching some basketball." That was partly true, he had watched Quinn and his friends play, that wasn't why he had been beaming from ear to ear, though.

Charles laughed. "You, sports?" He was in a nightshirt and a pair of sweatpants. Cody could smell the booze on him. His nose wrinkled, and bile rose up in his throat. Charles was always drinking. Cody couldn't remember the last time he hadn't smelled alcohol on the boy.

Cody remained quiet, deciding not to entertain his brother anymore. Charles was just looking for a reason to harass him, that was all. Charles grew frustrated and kicked him in his stomach. Air left Cody's lungs as he crouched over, lying in a fetal position as his brother aimed kick after kick at him.

A door creaked in the lit-up hallway, making the two boys look towards its entrance. No one came out, but their mother spoke up.

"What's going on out there? Charles?" Her voice came from her room, meaning that she must have Charles' slaps and kicks from her room. Charles' looked a bit shocked at the sound of her voice, he must have thought she was asleep. Charles looked down at Cody, giving him one last frown before stepping away from him.

"Nothing Ma," Charles said, before looking back at Cody who was still lying on the floor. "Get up," Charles muttered, kicking him again.

Cody got up and began to leap towards the hallway.

"Sleep in the living room, I don't want you in our room." Cody paused at the sound of his brother's words.

Cody sighed, nodding his head even though he was on the verge of tears. "Okay," he managed to let out without bursting into tears.

Charles walks past him, before disappearing into the dark hallway, leaving Cody alone in the dimly lit sitting room. He sighed, looking up when he heard the door to the bedroom that he shared with Charles slam close. He looked around the living room. The television was still flooding the room with colorful lights, and the noise coming from it filled what would have been the white noise left in Cody's head from the slap he'd received.

The boy licked his lips, bending down to pick up the remote he had dropped as he fell. He turned off the television, sucking the room of all light and sound. He could hear his heart spasm in his ears, and he had to open his mouth to let himself breath since his chest was heavy from the weight of the tears he was fighting not to shed. He walked over to the sofa, before crawling into it and turning his head to the side so that his face was buried in the backrest.

His skin felt hot. His cheeks were burning with fever-like warmth, and the pressure in his eyes caused by tears trying to make themselves visible was painful. He almost gave in to the sobbing—almost.

In the darkness, the frail boy smiled. He would have cried until he passed out if this had been any other day, but he had something—someone—to look forward to. It was a great feeling, and it made his heart race as images of the bronze-skinned looped smiling taller boy flashed through his mind.

"I've got Quinn," he whispered under his breath like he was afraid his brother would walk into the living room and demand to know who that was.

No, he wouldn't allow that at all. He was going to keep Quinn a secret. Charles wasn't going to mess this up for him too. Cody's hands squeezed into fists as he reprocessed what Quinn had asked him. He had asked him on a date. Just remembering that made him overwhelmingly happy, and for once in a very long time, Cody didn't cry himself to sleep while under his mother's roof.

CHAPTER FOURTEEN

C ody and Quinn had taken a bus a little out of their small town to go to the free-range farm animal petting zoo run by a group of farmers. It was late in the afternoon, and the sun shone down blinding rays. Cody and Quinn were hiding from the heat and brightness under one of the four canopies that were set up. They watched the peacocks wander about, pecking the ground for grains from under the shade.

Cody giggled, "It's beautiful." The boy looked at the bird that had walked close to them to pick at the feed they'd been pouring on the ground.

Quinn smiled, happy that Cody was having fun. "Yeah," he said, looking at the chickens in distance. When Cody had said yes to going on a date with him, he had been surprised, but he had clenched on to it. The next day he had been surprised to see Cody covered in bruises, but the smaller boy had smiled at him and asked when and where they would be going for the date, ignoring the fact that a section of his face was swollen and turning a nasty pink.

Quinn let himself turn to look at Cody. The smaller boy was grinning from ear to ear as a bird scavenged the soil close to him. The sight of his happiness made Quinn's face and ears grow warm. He was happy Cody was having so much fun. Going to the petting zoo had been something he had thought of last minute. He knew Cody liked animals, and he had some loose change to buy two entry tickets. After a while of them just standing under the shade they left it to walk around. When evening drew close the two boys left the petting zoo and started heading home.

"How was it?" Quinn asked when they got down from the bus and started on their half an hour walk home.

Cody smiled. "It was great!" His voice had a cute skip to it.

"I'm happy to hear that," Quinn said, stretching out his hand, and brushing Cody's arm with his fingertips. "Can I hold your hand? No one really uses this path, so there's nothing to worry about," Quinn said, feeling his voice tremble. He was still nervous about coming on to Cody. He wasn't sure where his feelings drew a line.

Cody stared down at Quinn's darker hand for a bit, before reaching out to hold it. He gave it a squeeze that made Quinn smile. The two continued to head on their way, hand in hand.

Cody's face grew warm with every passing second. Quinn's larger hand was warm and firm, and it made his smaller hand feel safe in its grasp. Quinn didn't let go of his hand even when they got to a more crowded area, but Cody didn't ask for him to let go of it. If Quinn was fine with people seeing them, he was fine with it too.

"We should get something to eat at the convenience store, how's that?" Quinn said when he noticed that they would soon have to part ways. He didn't want that. He wanted to spend as much time as possible with Quinn.

Cody nodded. "That sounds like a good idea." Quinn smiled, and with that, the two boys turned at the fork of the road to head to the nearby convenience store.

Quinn let go of Cody's hand at the door. "I'll be out soon," he promised.

"Okay," Cody muttered, watching as Quinn grinned before disappearing through the store's door. Cody waits at the side, resting his back on the wall.

Quinn, true to his word, was out in five minutes. "Here," he said, tossing a bottle of soft drink at Cody's direction.

The boy catches it. "Thank you," he said, looking over at Quinn who just grinned at him. The two went to the stairs at the back of the store to sit down. They sipped from their bottles in silence, not saying anything to each other as they watched the sun begin to set from their seats on the concrete staircase. They soon finished their drink, but none of them got up. They didn't want to part.

"You're smiling," Quinn said, making Cody turn and look up at him. He covered his cheeks, watching the grin on Quinn's face widen.

Cody's eyes flickered away from Quinn "Yeah," he muttered feeling his face warm up.

"I love it when you smile—when you seem happy." Quinn's voice made him look up at Quinn. The boy had a serious look in his face now. It felt intimidating—like Quinn would swallow him if he kept staring. Cody looked away, feeling overwhelmed by both the boy's words and his serious expression.

"Am I overdoing it?" Quinn asked after a while.

Cody frowned. "Overdoing what?" he asked, looking back at Quinn whose face was now dusted with a deep blush.

"The flirting thing. Am I coming off too strong?" Quinn asked, making Cody's face flush. The smaller boy didn't say anything in response. He just stared.

Quinn groans, rubbing the back of his neck. "I'm sorry, I just really like you, and I'm nervous. When I'm nervous I talk a lot."

A chuckle escaped Cody's lips. "It's okay."

Quinn rose a brow. "Are you sure?" he asked, cocking his head to the side to look at Cody.

"Yeah," the smaller boy confirmed, running his fingers through his hair. "Yeah, I don't mind if you flirt with me a lot."

Quinn sighed in relief. "Okay."

There was a pause that made Quinn uncomfortable, so he tried to crack the ice. "I'm new to this dating thing if you couldn't tell," Quinn said, letting out a low laugh. Cody chuckled too, but he didn't say anything, so the silence returned.

Quinn feeling nervous blurts the first thought that pops in his head, "Why did you say yes to going on a date with me? I'm sorry. You don't have to answer it if you don't want to. I was just wondering—"

"I like you," Cody said, cutting the taller boy off.

Quinn blinked, surprised at the blunt answer. "Oh." The silence from before came back, but Quinn itched to say something in response.

"I like you a lot, I guess you already know that," he muttered, laughing a little. He did that a lot—laughing when he was nervous.

"I thought I was going to burst from joy when you asked me on a date," Cody said, looking over at Quinn with a smile. "I really like you, and I didn't think you liked me..." he trailed, going quiet at his last sentence.

He muttered something Quinn couldn't hear under his breath as he fidgeted with his fingers. He let out a sigh. "I mean look at me—"

"What do you mean 'look at you'?" Quinn asked, reaching out to run his fingers through Cody's hair "You're very pretty. Is that weird to say? I don't think you're handsome—pretty, just very pretty." Quinn was blurting nonsense now.

Cody laughed. "I don't think that makes sense."

"Neither do I," Quinn admitted. The boys laughed, and somehow, they were sitting much closer—the space between them on the stairs gone. Quinn had moved down a stair, and now they were sitting side by side. The taller boy reached out for Cody's hand and the boy let him take it. They were holding hands now, both watching the orange of the sun disappear behind the grey of the clouds.

"Hey," Quinn said, making Cody turn to face him. "Would it be too much if I asked for a kiss?" Quinn's face grew warm as the request left his lips.

Cody shook his head. "No, not at all." He was nervous too, but he wanted Quinn to kiss him. He'd been thinking about that all week.

Cody could feel his heart beating faster as the dark-haired boy cupped his cheek with his hand before bringing his face forward. Their lips touched for a moment before the two pulled away. The kiss was light—almost nonexistent.

Quinn took in a deep breath. His heart was racing from the peck, but it didn't feel enough. He stared at Cody, gathering the courage to ask for another one, "Is it okay if I want to do it again—?" He paused. "For longer this time?"

Cody smiled. "Yes," he said reaching out to cup Quinn's face bin his hands before pressing his lips against the boy's. He moved his lips, opening his mouth a bit when Quinn touched his lips with his tongue. They sighed into each other's mouth, pressing and touching their tongues as their warm breaths fanned each other's face. Quinn hummed into the kiss, letting his fingers run through Cody's hair.

Quinn felt like his heart was going to burst. His stomach felt warm, and the hairs on his body stood up to every whimper and sigh that came out of Cody's mouth. Cody felt overwhelmed by Quinn too. His hands shook so he wrapped his arms around Quinn and balled his hands into fists and Quinn kissed along his neckline. The boys continued to kiss on the stairs, holding on to each other as the sun set. None of them had ever felt the way they felt that evening before—the hungry want for another person's touch.

A specific person's touch.

CHAPTER FIFTEEN

Quinn and his mother were both in the kitchen. He was standing by the counter as he watched her cook. It was early in the afternoon on a weekend, and the fan above didn't really do much to counter how hot the place had become due to the steam coming out from the pot. Quinn's dad had work to do. He was a mechanic, and he fixed cars regardless of what day it was. Janet also had a meetup with some of her friends, which left Quinn and his mother alone by themselves.

It was the perfect time to tell her about Cody—to come out.

"Mum." Quinn's voice was small, but his mother heard him.

"Hmm?" she hummed, looking at him for her eyes before turning back to the pot in front of her. The stew was bubbling, and the blue-red flames on the cooking gas danced.

Quinn felt his voice get stuck in his throat. You need to tell her. He scolded himself in his head as his heartbeat against his ribcage. He wasn't sure why he was panicking. At worst his mother would be disappointed, but she wouldn't throw him out or ban him from seeing Cody. He knew that. His mother was a 'mind your business' Catholic. She didn't pull him or his father by the ear to follow her to church, and she stayed away from Janet's love life. Quinn had just expected her to be a little more reactive.

"Remember Cody?" he asked, hoping that she caught on to the fact that the boy had been coming over a lot lately. Quinn even helped him keep some clothes in his room.

"He's little. My age, but small looking. He's also kind of pale," Quinn rambled, running his fingers through his hair.

"The boy you keep bringing over?" she asked, turning to look at her son. The mother's brown eyes held her son's darker ones. They stared at each other for a bit, before Quinn looked away from her and nodded.

"Okay, what about him?" The sound of a bubbling liquid filled the air the same time warm mist rose. Quinn looked up, smelling the soup. His mother had turned away from him to stir the stuff in the pot.

"I—" Quinn's words paused at the bridge of his mouth. They were too scared to pass through. Too scared of getting that sad disappointed look his mother gave him when she wasn't pleased with whatever he had done. Most of them were for causing trouble with Kyle about the neighborhood, being rude to some annoying adults or fighting with his sister. Quin wondered if liking a boy was high or low on the seriousness scale. He wasn't sure. All the times he heard about gay people it was done in whispers. Sometimes it was straight out disproving, and sometimes mixed or neutral.

Quinn wondered how his mum felt.

He needed to tell here.

"I like him," Quinn said, watching as his mother closed the pot and put away the spoon to turn and look at him. "I really like him," he emphasized when he had her full attention.

"Quinn?"

The boy blinked, realizing that tears had started to form in his eyes. He looked down at his hands and squeezed them into fists when he noticed they were shaking.

"Mum I like him," he said again. "I really like him," he repeated. He couldn't say more. Those were the extent of his explaining. What else could he say?

"Did you two fight?" Quinn heard his mother ask, and soon he was pulled into a hug that made him lean onto her chest. She smelled like spices and cheese. Quinn sneezed, feeling his eyes water again.

"No," Quinn mumbled into his mum's chest as wrapped his hands around his mum's back. They rocked from side to side. "Mum?" he called, and his mutter hummed, making her chest vibrate with the sound. "Did you understand what I mean?"

"You like him. That you probably kiss him a lot when he comes here. I understand," she said, and Quinn felt his chest ache. He pulled away from her chest, looking for that disappointed look he knew so well. It wasn't there.

Liking a boy was low on his mother's serious offenses lists, confirmed.

"Yeah..." he trailed, rubbing the back of his neck before looking down at the worn-out tiles. He had just told his mother that he liked a boy. and all she'd done was hug him tight and ask him if they'd had a fight. He hadn't expected the worst, but this was more than he had hoped for.

"What do you like about him?" His mum asked, reaching out to pinch his cheek. "What about him has you acting like a puppy?" she asked, referring to how Quinn babied Cody when he came over.

"He's so small..." Quinn said the first words that popped out of his head. Of course, there were other reasons, but Cody being so cute was high up on his list.

"Then I'm not very sure he ate well as a kid," Quinn's mum said in response to his description of Cody. She had seen him from afar a couple of times when she walked in late, and sometimes she gave him food. The boy was quiet, and he didn't talk much, so she wondered how he got involved with her son who was all over the place and noisy.

Quinn chuckled, rolling his eyes before taking his mum's hand away from his face. "Don't say that about him, mum, that's rude."

"What? It's probably true. Malnutrition is a thing," she said, walking back to the kitchen counter beside the stove. She started dicing onions on the chopping board again.

Quinn sighed, walking a bit closer to his mum so that he was peering over her shoulder. "I guess you're right."

"Is something the matter?" she asked, turning to touch her boy's forehead. "Is there something on your mind?"

"No," Quinn said, frowning. "Yes." He ended up confessing.

"What is it then?" his mother asked,

Quinn nibbled on his lower lip. "Cody doesn't really like staying at home—"

"Family issues?" his mother said, cutting him off.

Quinn took a deep breath before sighing, "Yeah."

The two of them stopped talking, and the sound of the water boiling in the pot on the stove, as well as the sound of Quinn's mother chopping up foodstuff for the stew, she wanted to prepare replaced the sound of their voices in the void.

"Issues like that are common, but, well, at least now he has you," Quinn's mother said as she peeled the purple skin of another onion.

Quinn smiled a bit. "I guess." The two stopped talking for a bit, and the only sound that filled the room was that of the knife hitting a chopping board, and the occasional sound of a passing vehicle through the living room window.

"Do you want me to dice some carrots for you?" Quinn's mother asked. Quinn's lips broke out into a grin as he nodded, making his dark hair bounce with the action. His mother did as she promised and handed him a bowl freshly of diced carrots.

"Here."

Quinn takes the bowl from her, before dipping his hand into it to grab a handful to shove in his mouth. He walked back a bit before he was leaning on the counter adjacent to the stove. Quinn's mouth was full as he chewed. He watched as his mum poured the diced ingredients into the pot from time to time before stirring.

"Does Cody eat well at school? Does he bring in lunch?" Quinn's mother asked out of the blue.

Quinn frowned, trying to think. "Now that I think about it, not really. He mostly eats just snacks." Snacks that he bought himself. Quinn doubted he had an allowance of any sort.

Quinn's mum nodded. She had expected that. "Will he mind if I made some food for him from time to time?"

"I don't think he'll mind. He'll probably be grateful, he seems to like your cooking," Quinn said.

His mum turned to smile at him. "I'll start doing that then," she said as she rubbed her hands dry on the apron she was wearing. Quinn smiles back at his mum and tried his best to keep his food in his mouth when his mother tickled his neck as she made to get something from the cupboard by the counter.

"Have you been to his place?" she asked him, returning to the kitchen counter by the stove with the can of sweet corn in her hands.

Quinn shakes his head "No, not exactly." He shrugs. "I've walked him home, but I've never been inside his house. I haven't seen his mum or brother either."

Quinn's mother's smile falls a bit. "Ah, that's too bad. I wanted to see if I knew his family. What about his surname?"

"Bell," Quinn said, remembering the boy's full name from what he has scribbled on his notebook.

Quinn's mother sucked in her cheeks, and in an almost sing-song voice repeated, "Bell. Bell. Bell." She sighed. I haven't heard of it. They're new here though, so that's expected. "I would have asked you where his mum works, but I'm sure you don't know that."

"Yeah, I don't," Quinn confirmed.

There was silence.

"You're going to play basketball today, aren't you?" Quinn's mother asked.

"Yeah," he said, dropping the now-empty bowl of carrot in the sink. His face was growing warm. It was a Sunday, but Cody had said that he would maybe drop by. Since their first kiss, they had started kissing a lot, and with every time one of them would be bold enough to do something new. It had been embarrassing to touch under each other's shirt, and it had also been embarrassing to grind their lower halves—but the feeling had been temporary and had given way to new waves of excitement.

Quinn's mother smiled. "If Cody's out there you can invite him for dinner, or just ask him what he likes to eat since I want to make something for him."

Quinn smiled at his mother before resting his hands on the counter. "Yeah, I'll do that," he muttered, making his mom smile. The two of them continued to talk, and their conversation distracted them until Quinn had to leave.

CHAPTER SIXTEEN

As Quinn and Cody grew closer, Quinn started to follow him every at school. At first, they had kept their distance, apart from lunch, but Quinn decided he would shadow Cody when he noticed some of the boys in their year picking on him. People stared. They stared more than they did during launch when Quinn would work over to sit with the boy.

Quinn's friends had gotten used to him heading over to look for Cody. It had moved from the strange to the slightly odd thing that happened occasionally. They were clueless about the boy's crush aside from Karl and Hozier who found out when the three of them had walked home together and Karl had blurted it out.

"You like a boy?" Hozier had asked that evening on their walk. Quinn had just nodded his head, waiting for the worst. "Sorry if any of the gay jokes weren't funny to you," was Hozier said. Quinn had looked up, smiling at his friend. They were rascals, but they were good people inside.

"But why him though?" Hozier had asked and Quinn had just shrugged. Seeing Cody at the court all the time had sparked a curiosity in him and learning more and more about Cody had only made him grow closer to the boy. He hadn't been that interested in anyone in his life, and it had just felt right. He didn't tell all of that to Hozier though. He had just given him a punch while Karl laughed—his voice mixing with the sound of dogs barking in the distance.

"Are you going to see twinkle toes today?" Quinn snapped out of his thoughts, turning to look at Karl who had whispered into the ear. It was the last period on a Tuesday, and all Quin could think about was walking home with Cody. He smiled, nodding his head, making Karl sigh and roll his eyes.

"Whatever," Karl said, moving his focus to his textbook.

When the final bell rang, and the school hours ended, Quinn went to find Cody, and soon the both were on their way home together—their fingers slightly touching as they walk through the long, but quiet path together. Shadows from the trees reflected on the path, dancing and shifting as the leaves and position of the sun changed.

"Tell your mum I said thanks for the food. It was great," Cody said, staring down and watching his sneakers thread on the dirt path.

"Sure thing," Quinn said, smiling as he poked the inside of Cody's palm. The boy pulled away, looking at Quinn with a frown for a bit before bursting into laughter.

"What? What are you laughing at?" Quinn asked, raising a brow at Cody.

Cody grinned, before reaching out to grab and squeeze Quinn's hand. "Nothing. I'm just happy."

Quinn felt his face heat up. He looked up ahead, not wanting Cody to tease him for being flustered. "That's good to hear."

The two boys continued to walk together until they got to an abandoned shack they stopped by often. They made to sit on the stairs, and they talked about everything and nothing as time passed them by.

"Maybe you should start making an actual appearance on the basketball court?" Quinn suggested after they talked about the game Quin had today.

Cody shook his head before covering his face with his hands. "No, I don't think so."

Quinn sighed, leaning forward. "Are you still afraid of my friends?" he asked, and Cody shrugged his shoulders, refusing to say anything.

Quinn's lips turned downwards. He sighed. "Whenever you're ready then." He forced himself to smile, before reaching to squeeze Cody's shoulder.

"Thanks," Cody muttered under his breath. He was wearing a long sleeve top and a pair of knee-length cargo shorts—Quinn's clothes. The two sat in silence until Quinn spoke up.

"Is Lindsey still bothering you?" Quinn asked.

Cody turned to look at Quinn before shaking his head. "Not really."

Lindsey had been pestering Cody since Quinn and Cody started hanging out together. She'd mostly taunt him with crude questions, and that was all there was to it. She still seemed upset about Quinn not dating her and had put one and two together about him and Cody.

Quinn sighed. "Good." He used his fingers to brush Cody's hair off his face He still hadn't cut it. "Don't take her seriously, okay. She's just jealous."

"I won't," Cody said. It was hard not to. Lindsey was pretty and everything most boys would want in a girlfriend, and sometimes Cody grew self-conscious. It was typical for people to tell their friends when they could do better, and he wondered if Quinn's friends would do that if they found out who he was asking on dates and kissing. He hid from Lindsey, and he hid from Quinn's friends too.

"Hey," Quinn started, making the smaller boy look at him. "My sister is a hairstylist you know. She could cut your hair," Quinn muttered and Cody blushed, nodding his head.

"Okay," he said as Quinn took his hand away. The two boys stared at each other as the conversation faded away.

Quinn frowned a bit, confusing Cody. "I always want to kiss you. Is that normal?"

Cody's eyes widened. He opened his mouth to say something, but his words got caught up in his throat. He looked away when his face grew warm with embarrassment.

Quinn chuckled at how cute the boy was being. "Honestly, though. I really like you," he said, and Cody looked up at him again.

Quinn's eyes narrowed at Cody's face. His heart ached at the sight of the bruise just under his lips. He knew how that happened. There had just been a silent agreement not to talk about Cody's wounds. "We're not dating or anything—I think, but you can tell me anything. I don't know, your happiness kind of matters to me now." Quinn let out a nervous laugh, wondering if he'd crossed a line.

Cody didn't day say anything, he just looked away, staring down at his worn-out sneakers.

Quinn bent forward so that he's on the same level as Cody's face. "Hey, am I making you uncomfortable?"

Cody raised his head, shaking it before sighing. "No. I just don't know what to say—"

"You don't have to say anything you don't want to. It's okay," Quinn said, cutting the boy off. Cody smiled, and the two sat in silence for a while. Cody listened to Quinn breathe. He watched the boy's tan face and full lips. His heart started to beat, still in disbelief that this person had chosen him—had asked him on a date and kissed him. Cody felt his face warm-up, so he looked away from Quinn.

"Hey," Quinn said, breaking the silence. Cody raised his head to look at him. He cocked his head, noticing the nervous look on Quinn's face.

"Hmm?" The boy hummed, waiting for Quinn to say something.

Quinn goes quiet for a while as he racked his brain for what to say. "What are we?" He'd wanted to be roundabout with his question, but he decided to be straight forward was the best.

Cody stared at Quinn, feeling his face warm-up before he looked away. There was a pause before words left his lips. "Whatever you want," he said.

Quinn could hear his heart beating in his ears. "Really? Whatever I want?" he asked, hoping that Cody knew what that meant.

"Yeah." Cody smiled at Quinn.

"Boyfriends?" Quinn said, and Cody nodded.

"Yes," the smaller boy said. Quinn could feel his heart spasm. His face was hot and his chest was squeezing up.

Quinn was still in disbelief. "So, you'll date me?"

Cody rose a brow at the taller boy, laughing at the situation. "I thought I already said yes?" he said, and Quinn's face grew warmer.

Quinn looked away from him, trying to calm his beating heart. "I-I was just checking," he said. Cody rolled his eyes, before resting his head on Quinn.

The two boys got up from the concrete stairs soon after before continuing their journey home. The two were a bit flushed, their fingers casually brushing as they walked in close proximity. Something had changed—the atmosphere felt lighter, and their moods seemed bright. A word had done that—glued them to each other.

Just before Cody got to the front door of his house, he tugged Quinn's hand, leading the taller boy to the small backyard. That had buckets and a few crates of empty beer stacked at the side.

Quinn frowned in confusion when Cody took a hold of his face. "What is it?" he asked, wondering if Cody wanted to ask him something.

Cody just smiled a bit, pulling Quinn's face down until their lips met. Quinn sighed into his mouth, pressing his tongue against Cody's as the two boys kissed in the safety of the evening shade.

Quinn was smiling ear to ear. "I liked that," he said, before staring at Cody. He felt a tug in his lower stomach, and his face grew hotter. "Again...?" he asked, staring into Cody's doe brown eyes.

Cody nodded, grinning before pulling Quinn into a kiss again. His lips were warm, although chapped a bit. Quinn let his fingers run through Cody's hair, before pulling the boy closer to him by pressing against his lower back. Cody took a few steps back until he was leaning on the wall.

They kept kissing, letting their hands wander under each other's shirts. Cody could feel Quinn's heart beating under his hands, and Cody stood still as Quinn's fingers lingered on his lower stomach. There was a funny gasp from Cody when Quinn let his fingers tugged at the belt holes on Cody's cargo shorts.

"That tickles," Cody explained and Quinn stared at Cody with wide eyes before bursting into laughter. Cody did the same. The sound of their chuckling was drowned out by the sound of birds chirping and a neighborhood dog barking.

The two of them had never felt the swirl of emotions within them before. Quinn felt full, like his patterned monotonous life was finally interesting and lively—Cody was filling the emptiness. Cody felt happy—truly happy for the first time in his life.

CHAPTER SEVENTEEN

The living room/kitchen of Quinn's apartment was filled with the smell of spices and cooked meat. It's late noon, and the family, along with Cody who'd been invited for dinner were sitting about and eating rice from their plates as they talked.

Quinn's mother narrowed her eyes at Cody. "Eat up, we must do something about how small you are."

The boy blushed, making Quinn groan.

"Mum, stop it," he said, looking over at Cody with soft eyes to see if he was okay. Quinn's mother laughed, looking away from them.

Quinn whispered under his breath. "You can have as much or as little as you want," he said, still worrying about what his mother had said.

Cody smiled, nodding at his boyfriend before reaching out for the bowl across the living room's center table.

Quinn's mother spoke up, starting a conversation. "So, what do you plan to do after graduation? Trade? Most of the boys in your year are doing a trade." She said, looking at Cody. The boy remained silent, and his brows knitted together. He hadn't considered any of that. He'd just been thinking about waking up the next day—alive.

Quinn's mother looked away, poking at the piece of pork on her plate. "I'm guessing you haven't decided yet," she said, and Cody nodded,

Janet laughed from the other end of the table, catching Cody's attention. "You're so quiet," she said. It wasn't malicious, she had a smile on her face, and looked amused if anything. That didn't stop Quinn at glaring at her, though.

"Leave him alone," he said, shooting daggers at his sister.

The older girl raised her hands in defeat "I'm sorry," she said with a chuckle.

Quinn's father was quiet throughout the scene. He was reading a newspaper at the kitchen counter and ended up talking to Quinn's mother for the most part of the evening. Quinn hadn't come out to him—his mother had done that for him. His father hadn't been rude or cruel, but he didn't talk to Quinn much these days, and the atmosphere was generally uncomfortable when it was just the two of them.

Eventually, Quinn's mum and dad left the living room/Kitchen, leaving Janet, Cody, and Quinn by themselves. The three had put on the T.V. after cleaning up after themselves. The movie they were watching was an old one from over twenty years ago that Quinn's dad had on a VHS tape that managed to survive several moves.

The two boys cuddled on the couch, while Quinn's sister sat on one of the wooden chairs on the small dining table by the kitchen.

Quinn looked down at Cody who had his head on Quinn's shoulder. He hadn't said anything in a while, and Quinn wondered if he was feeling well.

"Is something wrong?" he asked, brushing some hair away from Cody's face.

Cody shrugged. "I have to head back soon," he mumbled, his voice just high enough for Quinn to pick up.

"Oh," Quinn said, looking back at the colors dancing on the television screen. His throat felt numb. He knew how much Cody hated going back home.

"You can sleep over if you want. It's the weekend after all." He offered, hoping Cody would consider it.

Cody's eyes flickered up at Quinn. "They'll wonder where I am—"

"You can do what you did the last time you were here. You can sleep here, then I'll wake you up early in the morning so you can go back home, how does that sound?" Quinn said, cutting the boy off.

Cody sucked on his cheeks as he proceeded to think about the offer. His mother didn't really care where he was, and it was just Charles that would harass him for being out late at night—but Charles would beat him up either way. He might as well stay over. He didn't want to go home, and his brother might be up at this time just to taunt him when he got back. Somehow, Charles had picked up on the fact that Cody wasn't just wondering about the streets but was meeting up with someone.

"Okay..." Cody said after hesitating for a bit.

Quinn looked down at Cody, smiling. He felt a bit better knowing Cody wasn't going back home to get a few more bruises on his face. He touched the newest one, just below his chin. They didn't talk about anything else and sat together on the couch until the movie ended.

"Oh, he's staying over," Janet said, letting her eyes follow Quinn and Cody as they made to leave the living room for Quinn's bedroom when they were done putting things away.

"Yeah," Quinn said, smiling at his sister who was giving him an equally big grin. She rolled her eyes before looking away, her hands bringing out the novel she'd been reading up to her face.

Cody and Quinn walked through the hallway, and Cody hugged himself as Quinn opened the door to his bedroom before pushing it forward.

"Come in," Quinn said, taking Cody's hand before leading him to the small closet bedroom. He let go of him when they reached the center, before going to search his drawer for something he and Cody could change into.

"Here," he said, turning to toss a pair of shorts and a tank top at Cody. Cody caught it, before heading to the other end of the room to change. It didn't matter how many times he slept over. Sharing Quinn's clothes and bed and changing in front of him always made Cody nervous.

He fumbled a lot when trying to get into the clothes, but Soon CODY was in the clothes Quinn had lent to him.

Quinn had wandered over to his bed. He waited for Cody to join him, but the boy just stood awkwardly in the corner. Quinn rose a brow at him. "Do you want to sleep standing?" He said, laughing a bit. Cody's eyes widened and he looked down at the floor.

"No-no," he stuttered, holding on to his arm as a blush crept up his face.

"Then come here," Quinn said, tapping the space beside him on the mattress. The lights in the room where dim.

Cody stared at Quinn for a bit before heading to join him on the bed. He sat down on the edge first, before pulling his legs on the bed and laying down. He faced Quinn, staring into the boy's eyes.

"See, isn't this better than standing?" Quinn asked, laughing as he touched Cody's face with his fingers.

"Shut up," Cody said, still embarrassed, but that didn't stop him from scooting closer to Quinn. They cuddled, and the two boys' legs tangled together as they held onto each other.

Quinn stopped laughing. A smile made its way to his face as he looked into Cody's deep brown eyes. "You said something, finally," he muttered, watching as Cody's eyes flickered away from his as his face got dusted with a baby pink color.

"Shut up..." Was the only thing Cody could manage, and it made Quinn chuckle before pulling the boy closer to his chest. Cody could hear Quinn's rapid heartbeat, and he took comfort in the fact that it meant he wasn't the only one that was nervous.

They talked, periodically falling into silence until one person took the chance to kiss the other. Their hands wandered as usual—under each other's shirts, between each other's thighs, on their hips and waists.

"Quinn..." Cody's voice was small, but Quinn heard him. He kissed the boy's forehead, still letting his hand brush over the front of the boy's shorts. "Quinn..." the boy trailed again when Quinn let himself pull-down Cody's shorts before dipping his hand into his boxers. Cody let out a low mewl, and he shivered at the feel of Quinn's hand on his bare skin.

"Quinn..." he trailed again, shutting his eyes closed as the taller boy wrapped his fingers around him, and slowly stroked.

"What?" Quinn asked, pressing a kiss to the boy's forehead and he moved closer, the hardness between his own thighs brushing Cody's leg. "Do you want to ask me something?" he added when Cosy didn't say anything.

"N-no, don't," he stuttered, closing his eyes as his breathing hiked. Quinn was still touching him—slowly, gently, with love. "It just feels a bit w-weird," he said, gasping when Quinn rubbed a finger over his tip. His legs spasmed again, and he felt his lower stomach tighten up.

"Weird?" Quinn asked, getting confused. He let go, and Cody shook his head, pressing up against him.

"Not weird as in weird," he tried to explain, looking down between them as he tried to come up with the proper words. It felt good. Really good. He reached his hands down, tracing Quinn's hardness through his clothes. "I mean, kind of surreal. I want it to happen, but it feels like a dream somehow..." Cody trailed, feeling his face warm up as he realized he had in a way, told Quinn that he dreamt about things like this.

"You dream about stuff like this?" Quinn asked after a while of extended silence as he kissed Cody's neck.

"Y-yes," the boy admitted, shivering as he managed to pull Quinn's pants down a bit. The boy's privates popped out and a shot of excitement flooded Cody's bloodstream. "Quite a bit."

"How about you?" Cody asked when Quinn didn't say anything. Cody knew that all this was quite new to Quinn. As popular as the boy was, he was naive to stuff like this. Cody didn't want to feel like a pervert about his thoughts.

"I do, but it's kind of rude..." Quinn mumbled, and Cody frowned a bit.

"Rude?" he asked, and Quinn squirmed, hiding his face in the pillow.

"The things I imagine you doing, I don't think you'd want to do them," Quin explained as Cody's hand kept stroking him.

"Like what?" the smaller boy asked, wanting to hear him say it.

"W-would you... suck on me if I asked?" Quinn asked, and Cody's face warmed up.

"Yeah..." he trailed. He imagined that a lot. He wanted to do that, and he wanted Quinn to do it for him too. Sometimes just looking at the boy's full lips had his stomach in a knot. "Would you do it for me?" he whispered back.

"Yeah," Quinn mumbled, shuddering as Cody kept stroking him. He reached out too, touching Cody and continuing where he had left off. The two boys closed their eyes, sighing as they touched each other.

"Hey," Cody mumbled, opening his eyes. Quinn's eyes peeled open too and there were staring at each other. "Do you think you could fuck me?" Cody didn't get an answer to that because Quinn came in his hand, letting out a little whimper before burying his face in the nearest pillow. Seeing Quinn so flustered made Cody come too. The two boys hugged each other, squirming a bit at the stickiness between them.

"Why would you say it like that?" Quinn asked in a whisper. "Almost gave me a heart attack," he added, and Cody chuckled.

"Well," the smaller boy started. "Would you?" he asked, and Quinn nodded.

"We'll have to figure out how first," he mumbled, and Cody hummed in agreement. Cody had an idea, but scraps and pieces he'd picked up from discarded gay magazines weren't a full picture.

The two boys slept off soon after, dreaming about the other without embarrassment or shame.

CHAPTER EIGHTEEN

The next morning Cody had woken alone on the bed. He sat up, looking down to see that someone had cleaned him up. He narrowed his eyes at his thighs, only putting two and two together when the door to the bedroom creaked open and Quinn walked in.

"Sorry, we woke up late," Quinn trailed, tossing the towel on his shoulder on his drawer before kneeling to look through it for clothes. "The bathroom is empty. You should go take a shower before someone else gets in," Quinn muttered.

Cody nodded. "Yeah, I'll do that," he muttered, getting out of the bed before grabbing Quinn's towel and leaving for the bathroom. He brushed his teeth at the sink with the toothbrush Quin had given him one of the nights he'd slept over. Since then the brush hadn't left the family cup. Four brushes, and the weird cheap one that Quinn had managed to fish out for Quinn. Cody smiled at the thought. It felt like this was his home now in a sense. He slept over a lot, and he ate more food here than he did when he was at home.

What if I lived here? He wondered, looking at himself in the mirror. He shook his head before rinsing his mouth. No, he couldn't. That would be taking Quinn and his family's kindness for granted.

When he got back to Quinn's bedroom there were already clothes laid out for him. He wore them and followed the smell of toast and bacon to the Kitchen/living room where Quinn was waiting for him on the small dining table. They didn't talk much, but they gave each other looks. Quinn helped Cody butter his toast, and Cody helped Quinn finish off his mug of hot chocolate when he couldn't. It was still early in the morning, so the rest of the family wasn't up yet.

"What my mum said," Quinn started, looking over at Cody was they both took care of the dishes at the sink. "About what you'll do after graduation..." Quinn trailed and Cody looked away.

"I don't know what I'll do," Cody mumbled. He would eighteen soon, and Charles would use that as a reason to kick him out that's for sure. His anxiety and general battered look hadn't made it easy to get a part-time job of any sort. He didn't have experience. Going to school was even worse. He had nothing he liked about it.

"That's okay, we'll figure it out together," Quinn said, drying off the last bowl before putting it away.

The two left the apartment complex together. Quinn wasn't with his school supplies because it was still early in the morning, he just wanted to escort Cody home so that he could get his stuff. They had woken up late, so Quinn couldn't drop him off just before the break of dawn like they had planned.

The sound of dogs barking and birds singing filled the streets. The sun peeked from the horizon, shining rays of yellow light on the dirt floor. Cody and Quinn's hands separated when they reached the flat Cody lived in with his family. They were both anxious for what they knew would happen when Cody went in.

"I'm sorry..." Quinn trailed when Cody reached out to tug at his shirt. The smaller boy was afraid to go in. The reality had only hit him when the house had come in full view of them as they approached it. However, it seemed quiet. The lights were off and there was no one hanging around the compound, although Charles' motorcycle was parked by the stairs.

"It's not your fault we woke up late," Cody said, giving his boyfriend a smile. He didn't regret it. He waved Quinn off before heading to the front door.

The boy slipped into the living room of the home he shared with his brother and mother, his heartbeat picked up as he looked about for any sign of his brother or mother. He let out a sigh of relief when he didn't either of them before taking a seat on the couch.

The relief was short-lived because a door in the hallway creaked open, and Cody's eyes widened as he turned towards the hall to see his brother walk out of the entrance.

"Don't think I didn't notice you were gone. You didn't come home yesterday, did you?" the older boy said, walking up to the sofa Cody was sitting on. "Where were you?" Cody remained quiet, lowering his head instead.

He heard his brother groan "Answer me you piece of shit."

"I—I was at a friend's place." Cody managed to get out. He heard his brother laugh.

"Friend? As if you have friends," he said, walking behind the couch. Cody bit his lower lip, forcing his gaze to focus on the carpet below so that he wasn't tempted to look at his brother.

"There's only one thing you could be good at, and that's being a slut. Look at me before I knock your teeth off. You're even wearing a different set of clothes—disgusting," Charles said, breaking Cody's restraint. The smaller boy looked up at his brother but bit down on his tongue so that he didn't say anything in response.

Cody's brother was bulky and dark-haired, but they didn't look the same. He had a smirk on his face that told Cody he wasn't going to leave the scene without giving him a bruise or two.

"My mother could have left you. She could have abandoned the son of slut that stole her husband, but she didn't, be grateful," The older boy said, frowning down at Cody.

Cody could feel tears building up in his ducts. Grateful? At first, he had been, but after suffering years of physical and mental abuse, he wasn't sure what he should be grateful for anymore.

Cody's brother remained quiet for a while, and Cody even though he left until he felt a sharp pain from having his hand yanked and being pulled to a standing position. "You don't deserve to even sit down. You disgust me," Charles said as Cody blinked back tears.

Cody remained silent even though his hand felt like it was shattering from his half-brother's grip. Cody winched when his brother's grip only tightened.

Cody gasped. "Charles, please—"

"Don't use my name you piece of shit. Don't say my name, don't say my mother's name. I'm not your brother, and she's not your mother," Charles said, cutting the boy off before he could finish.

Cody gasped, staying quiet and biting down on his lower lip to avoid crying out. His arm hurt so much.

"When you're eighteen you'll be leaving this house and us. You won't get to annoy me by simply existing, and my mum doesn't have to remember the woman that stole her husband by simply looking at you—" Charles said, pausing as he yanked Cody some more, pulling the boy so that he stepped towards him.

Cody yelled, unable to endure the pain anymore. "Shit—"

"Shut up. You killed my father," Charles said, cutting him off. Cody's mouth was filled with blood from the force of biting down on his lip.

He swallowed, his eyes wincing from the taste of iron in his blood. He was going to pass out if Charles didn't stop. "I didn't do anything—"

"Your mum killed my father. What's the difference? If she hadn't made him move in with her, he wouldn't have been there when her house burned down," Charles said, squeezing Cody's arm until his skin was red and wrinkled under his grip. "The fact that you survived that day is a slap to my mum. It's like your mum's trying to live through you to mock us."

Charles let go of Cody when the boy coughed up blood. The smaller boy fell to the ground. He knelt, bending over and cradling his throbbing arm.

"Stay out of my way today. If I see you, I'll beat you up," Charles warned. Cody nodded through the pain. He closed his eyes and only knew Charles had left when the footsteps faded, and a door slammed shut.

The tears in Cody's eyes overflowed and Cody soon found himself bawling on the living room carpet. It wasn't the pain from his twisted hand. He was just tired of living and being a walking reminder of his mother. He felt sorry anytime he looked at Charles' mother. The woman didn't even look him in the eyes, and she never seemed interested in stopped Charles. In a way, she might have wanted to see Cody get punished a bit.

He was just so, so tired of simply existing and not living.

His throat hurt from crying and curling up into a ball didn't help. His mind instinctively thought of Quinn. It was still early, and maybe the boy hadn't left for school yet... No. He scolded himself in his head, not wanting to get Quinn mingled up in this. He remained on the floor for longer, feeling his hand throb and his boy convulse.

Quinn would want you to go to him. A voice said in his head between the pain. He'd want you to go to him, now.

Cody sighed, taking deep breaths as he sat up. His eyes narrowed at the front door, and his chest tightened. Yes, Quinn would want him to go to him, and Cody gave in, deciding that he should. Asking Quinn for help was not him being a nuisance. He got to his feet. They were wobbly, but he managed to walk well enough to make it out of the flat's front door.

Quinn. Was the only thought that remained in his mind as he walked through the streets barefooted with an aching arm and a clogged throat from crying.

CHAPTER NINETEEN

Cody was standing at the front door of Quinn's apartment door. He had somehow made it to the apartment complex, before climbing the stairs to the six-floor. He followed Quinn home a lot, so he knew what door. The '63' plate on it was one he'd stared at a lot as Quinn fished for his keys. The hallway was noisy. It was drowned in gospel music, T.V. noises, and babies crying. The noise from each apartment slipped through the spaces under doors and cracks on walls.

Cody held on to his stomach, feeling dizzy. His feet ached. His arm ached. Everything ached.

Cody had run all the way to Quinn's place without a second thought after he had convinced himself that he wouldn't be a burden to the boy, but now he was facing the door he wasn't sure if he should knock. He didn't want to be a bother. He didn't want Quinn to see him like this.

His head shot up when the door creaked open, not letting him make that decision for himself.

"Don't worry, I'll be back soon. I'm just — Cody?" Quinn's sister, Janet says as she looked straight at Cody. Hair eyes flickered from one bruise to the other, before settling on the hand he was cradling. "What happened?

Who the fuck did this to you?" she asked, her voice getting higher with every successive word.

There was a shout from the inside, and Janet looked behind her to tell her mum not to worry. She turned back to Cody, horrified at the dried blood on his shirt and the ugly bruise forming under his left eye and jaw. Quinn had told her that Cody didn't have a great family relationship, but he hadn't told her how terrible it was.

Cody could feel the tears in his eyes sting. He opened his mouth to say something, but he didn't know where to start or what to say. He hated Charles, but he didn't want to get the boy in legal trouble. Instead, he let out a small whisper, wincing at the numb feel zapping through his scalp.

"Should I get Quinn?" Janet asked as her anger gave way to the concerned look on her face as well as a soft voice.

Cody stared at her before looking down at the hallway tiles. "Y-yes," he stuttered, nodding his head as tears dripped from his eyes.

Janet gave him a forced smile. "I'll be right back," she muttered, disappearing behind the apartment's door.

After a few minutes of waiting, Cody watched as Quinn emerged from the apartment. He didn't have a chance to look at him properly or say anything before the taller boy embraced him in a hug. It was tight, but it was gentle—Quinn avoided pressing against his wounds.

"I have to head out, I'll leave you two to it," Janet said, giving Cody's shoulder a light squeeze before brushing past them. She looked late, and Cody felt a bit sorry for showing up out of nowhere.

The two boys stood in silence until the sound of Janet's shoes had faded into the distance as she took the stares down. Cody could feel his heart pound in his ears when Quinn took his good hand in his.

"What happened?" the taller boy asked, staring at Cody with concern. The smaller boy's eyes flickered away. He remained quiet, afraid to talk because he was sure he would meltdown and cry.

Quinn cocked his head after a while. "You don't want to talk about it?" he asked, pulling Cody into another soft hug.

The smaller boy nodded into his shoulder. "Yeah..." he trailed, sniffling a bit.

Quinn sighed, tightening his hold on Cody. "It doesn't matter. Tell me when you're ready. I'm always here for you, you know that, right?" Cody nodded into the boy's shoulder again as Quinn ran a hand through his hair. They stayed like that in the hallway for a bit, before Quinn pulled away from the hug.

"Come on, let's head inside," he said, giving his boyfriend a smile. It was forced, but he just had to be strong. Seeing Cody like this was hard. Very hard. He wanted to march all the way to Cody's house and beat the shit out of Charles, but he didn't want to do anything that would make Cody panic.

Cody nodded, giving Quinn a small smile before taking his hand and following the taller boy into his family apartment.

Quinn's mother greeted them, but she didn't turn away from the pot of food she was attending too. Quinn took the opportunity to lead Cody to his room, not wanting his mother to make a fuss of Cody's state. The boy's eyes were red from crying, his bruises were swollen, and he looked tired. She would leave soon, anyway, and Quinn didn't want her to be late for work.

Quinn had already decided he wasn't going to school today and was going to stay with Cody as he recovered.

When they both entered the room, Quinn started rambling. "Okay, what do you want to do? We could watch something on my phone, or we could talk—"

He was cut off when he felt slender arms wrap around his mid rift. There was silence as Cody hugged in, breathing deeply as he let out soft cries.

"Thank you," the smaller boy said as Quinn held on to the hands around him.

"For what?" Quinn asked in a small voice, hoping to get Cody to talk to him.

"Thank you," Cody repeated instead of answering the question. Where can I start? 'Thank you for liking me'? 'Thank you for reaching out to me when all I wanted to do was fade away'? Cody thought to himself. He wasn't sure how to put his thanks into words, so he just stayed silent right after.

Quinn didn't push for an explanation anymore and instead turned in the boys hold so that they were facing each other. The stared at each other in silence, watching each other's expression until Cody spoke up.

"I'm scared." the boy said as his eyes fluttered down.

"Why?" Quinn asked and Cody remains quiet as he reaches to pick at the lint on Quinn's shirt.

"I—" the boy started but paused. "I l-love you," he managed to get out, feeling his face warm up.

"I love you too," Quinn said, making Cody's eyes go wide. The smaller boy looked at Quinn, feeling his stomach tighten at the sight of the gentle smile on his face.

They were quiet, both hugging each other until Quinn pulled Cody away so that that the two of them could head to the bed to sit down. Quinn smiled at Cody, moving to hold the boy's jaw in his hands before leaning in to kiss him. The kiss was sweet—gentle, and it didn't matter to Cody if the inside of his mouth stung or if Quinn mistakenly pressed up against a bruise even though he was being gentle. Quinn was kissing him, and it made his heart sing. That was all that mattered.

Quinn pulled away from the kiss, frowning a bit at Cody. "You're scared because you love me?" he asked, trying to put one and two together from before.

"Yes—No. I just—I don't want us to break up and—I just want to be happy," Cody rambled, trying to explain himself as he fidgeted with his fingers.

Quinn smiled. Cody was just adorable. "I really love you, nothing like that will happen. I promise, okay?" Cody nodded before making to hug Quinn again.

After a while, Quinn pulled away. "I'm going to get a first aid kit," Quinn muttered, and Cody nodded, waiting for the boy. He came back and tended his wounds, and they shared words and kisses as Quinn dabbed Cody's bruises with cleaning spirits before bandaging them.

"Does your arm still hurt?" Quinn asked when he was done. He was kneeling on the floor by the bed.

"Yeah," Cody mumbled, looking down at Quinn. "But it feels better," he said, smiling. Quinn mirrored that smile before getting up and leaving the room again. He put the kit away, before returning to his room. Cody was lying down in bed now, so Quinn joined him cuddling up next to him.

"Hey, at least we get to miss school together," Quinn muttered. His mother had left before he had gone out to grab the cotton wool, bandages, and spirits, and she would be back long after he was expected to get back from school.

Cody smiled at that, humming as he cuddled up to Quinn who started stroking his hair.

The two boys ended up taking a nap on Quinn's bed, holding on to each other as morning gave way to afternoon, and afternoon gave way to the evening. Cody woke up before Quinn, and just took the time to stare at him—the person who made his heart dance—the person who was offering him a chance at happiness.

"I love you," Cody muttered under his breath, pressing his lips against Quinn's hairline in a shy kiss before pulling away to stare at him.

It was true. Cody did love Quinn very much.

CHAPTER TWENTY

It was a sunny afternoon in the school compound. Cody was in the backyard of the school building during the break. The noise from the main compound was muffled by the swaying leaves in the nearby shrubs. The boy was sitting on the concrete stairs that lead to the back door. Quinn hadn't come to school today due to a sudden fever, so Cody was feeling a bit out of place all alone.

It was strange. He was used to being alone, but since Quinn had started spending time with him in school it felt strange not to have him around. His anxiousness had led him not to each launch earlier in the afternoon, and he had stayed out of everyone's way to keep the attention off him.

"Do you know what happened to Quinn?" Karl had asked him, somehow managing to corner him in the bathroom. The boy had stared at Quinn's tall friend, finding it hard to find words to say.

"He was-s a bit si-ick..." Cody managed to let out, a bit afraid of the way Karl had his eyes narrowed at him. "I'm g-going to s-e-e him after school," he had added, looking down at the browning white tiles of the school's bathroom floor.

There had been a sigh, and then the sound of footsteps before a hand was placed on his shoulder. Cody had looked up to find himself eye to eye with Karl.

"I'm not going to eat you, man," he had laughed, squeezing Cody's shoulder before letting go. "I just wanted to know where Quinn was. He would beat my ass if I beat his boyfriend." Cody's eyes had widened at the last word, and Karl had just smiled at him.

"Treat him well," the taller boy had said before tucking his hands in his trouser pockets and wandering away.

A small hum left Cody's lips as he recalled the encounter. Karl had been nice, just like Quinn had said he would. He was starting to feel stupid about thinking that any of Quinn's friends were bullies. They were just big and rowdy. He guessed that sharing those traits with his stepbrother had wounded him mentally with anxiety around bigger people.

Cody was so deep in his thoughts that he hadn't heard the backyard gates rustling as they creaked open. He looked up when the person at the gates spoke up.

"Hey." The familiar female voice said, making Cody raise his head before narrowing his gaze at the backyard's entrance. His eyes widened when he spotted Lindsey walking into the backyard through the entrance that also served as an exit to the main compound. She had ditched her braids for natural short twists that bobbed around her round face. She was wearing sneakers, a small shirt, and a sweater that wasn't practical for the summer heat.

Lindsey looked over at Cody when she was completely inside the compound. The smile she flashed at him made Cody look away from her. "We need to talk." He heard her say as the sound of shoes crunching on sand

and glass got louder. When Cody looked up again Lindsey was hovering over him, standing by the stairs with her hands folded over her chest.

Cody remained quiet. He was afraid that if he said anything hid voice would choke up, so he just looked away. He heard Lindsey let out a sigh, and before he knew it the girl had taken a seat next to him on the stairs. They sat in silence for a bit, listening to the voice of students talking and joking in the main compound. Cody let himself look at her from the side of his eyes—observing her lean figure, pretty eyes, and symmetrical features. She was a little short of the girls in magazines, but they were edited beyond recognition anyway. This was who Quinn could have been dating.

"You really are the quiet type, aren't you? How many words do you say in a day in total, ten?" she muttered in a low voice, letting out a chuckle. Cody blinked, looking away but he could fight the urge to look at her, so he kept giving her glances from the corner of his eyes. He didn't say anything to respond to her. Yes, he was quiet. He heard it a thousand times from different people. Apparently, it was funny for some reason.

Lindsey sighed after a while of them sitting in silence. "I'm sure you can guess why I'm here."

"Quinn?" Cody muttered, turning to look at Lindsey. The girl nodded her head.

"Yup," she said, smiling a bit before adjusting the skirt she was wearing. "You're dating him, aren't you?" she said, placing her hands on her lap. Cody's eyes widened as his mouth hung open. He wasn't sure how she had picked up on that.

He nodded. "Y-yeah," he let out, feeling his face warm up.

Lindsey smiled a little, nodding her head. "I still don't understand why he's dating you. I mean, I don't get it? Even if he's into boys, why you? You can barely even talk." she said, making Cody feel taken aback. He looked away from her again before hugging his legs and leaning his head forward. Sure, all that was true, but he knew Quinn loved him sincerely.

Lindsey sighed, realizing she had let her jealousy take hold of her again. "I'm sorry for rambling, you can say I'm just in disbelief that's all." Cody looked at her from the side of his eyes and spotted her wearing a soft smile. He remains quiet, still, not wanting to engage with her.

Silence loomed over them for a bit and Cody busied himself with staring at the birds hopping from branch to branch on the nearby shrub.

"What happens after graduation?" Lindsey's question came out of nowhere. Cody blinked, turning to look at her.

"Hmm?" He wondered why she was talking about graduation. What did that have to do with anything?

Lindsey rolled her eyes at him, feeling he should know what she meant. "I mean, what happens when we've graduated. Will you two still be dating?" Cody looked down at his worn-out shoes, finally understanding where she was coming from.

The be honest, Cody had never thought of any of that. Sure, he knew Quinn would find some work or the other, but Cody wasn't sure about himself. His brother had vowed that he'd get thrown out of the house after graduation and thinking about what would come after that always scared him—so he didn't think. He just woke up every day deciding to push the thoughts of the future to the back of his mind.

"I don't know," Cody said, being honest. There was a pause Cody had expected Lindsey to fill, but when she didn't speak up, he looked over at her. "Why does it matter?" he asked with a raised brow.

Lindsey shrugged her shoulders. "I just asked, don't you see like, a future or something? Or don't you like Quinn—"

"I like him a lot," Cody said, cutting Lindsey off. "I love him," he added, watching as Lindsey's eyes widened.

The girl managed a smile even in her daze. "Well, maybe you should start thinking about the future then," she said before getting up from the staircase and dusting the back of her skirt.

"I have to go. See you around and say hello to Quinn for me when you see him after school," Lindsey said before making her way out of the backyard. Cody let out a sigh when she was gone. Interacting with her left him feeling a lot more mentally exhausted than he already was. Cody ran his fingers through his hair as his mind kept playing back the things that she had said to him.

Cody couldn't help but think that Lindsey had a point. It was only a few months until they were done with high school in general. Most of the students weren't going to college—people around their town didn't have the funds for that, but even though Cody was sure Quinn wouldn't get up and disappear from town one random morning, he was worried that he'd be forgotten as Quinn figured out what he wanted to do with his life.

The boy would grow up, and Cody would be stuck in the past.

"Plans..." Cody trailed under his breath. "Plans for the future," he said, frowning. He didn't even like the sound of the word 'future' coming out of his lips.

No matter how much he thought about it, he couldn't really think of anything he wanted to do in the future. He lived day by day, morning by morning, night by night. He had no plans. He'd never seen a reason to have them before, but maybe now he had to think up some because he was that if he didn't keep up with Quinn, he might end up being put aside.

Cody was brought out of his thoughts by the sound of the school bell ringing. He looked over at the back door, sighing before getting up and walking towards it, deciding that planning for the future could wait for another day.

PART THREE | FINDING THE WILL TO LIVE

P ART THREE

FINDING THE WILL TO LIVE

"To live is the rarest thing in the world. Most people exist, that is all."

—— Oscar Wilde.

CHAPTER TWENTY-ONE

C ody and Quinn were sitting on the stairs of the abandoned shack. Quinn was on the lower stair, while Cody was sitting on one higher up. The smaller boy was watching Quinn talk, but he got distracted and couldn't pick at what Quinn is saying as worry filled his thoughts. The sun was setting in the distance as the evening gave way for the night. The sound of birds and cars made a buzz at the back of his mind as he stared at Quinn's moving mouth.

"Cody? Is something wrong?" Cody blinks at the sound of Quinn calling his name. He looked down at the taller boy who now had a concerned frown on his face. He hadn't even noticed when he had stopped talking. "Is everything okay?" Quinn asked, and Cody nodded.

"Sorry, I was just thinking..." he trailed, running his fingers through his dark hair.

Quinn sighed, looking up at his boyfriend. "About what?" He asked, reaching to hold on to Cody's think leg through his faded blue jeans.

Cody shrugged. "Stuff," he said, not feeling like he was in the mood to talk.

"What sort of stuff?" Quinn probed, making Cody sigh.

"I don't know, stuff." Cody knew he was being rude, but he couldn't help himself. He'd been thinking a lot about what Lindsey had said to him, and he found it frustrating that he couldn't sort out his life on a schedule like most people seemed to be able to do.

Quinn sighed, pulling himself up from the lower stair to join Cody on the top one. He scooted close, making sure their thighs touched. "Come on, talk to me, please?" he begged, leaning forward so that he got a better look at Cody's face. The smaller boy had a slight frown on his face, and Quinn worried if he was annoying him.

Quinn poked at Cody's cheek. "You're frowning..."

Cody immediately forced himself to smile before raising his head. "I don't know. I'm not sure how to put in in words. I'm worried."

"About what?" Quinn asked, watching as Cody folded his hands on his lap.

Cody sighed. "The future."

"What about the future?" Quinn asked, reaching out to touch Cody's face.

Cody sucked in his breath, before rambling on. His words were a mirror of what Lindsey had told him to worry about. "About us. What happens after graduation? I'm been thinking about that for a couple of days—"

"We'll still be dating," Quinn said, cutting the boy off. He reached out to hold Cody's hand. "Well, unless you break up with me out of nowhere," he said, letting out a nerve filled laugh.

Cody blinked, sucking in his cheek "I don't think I'll be allowed to still stay at my house after graduation—"

Quinn cut him off. "Then just come stay with my family. They like you. We can share my room—"

Cody laughed, shaking his head. "I'm not sure I can just move into your house like that—"

Quinn laughed before Cody could finish. "Why not?" he asked, smiling at his boyfriend. "You can," he added, giving his hand a squeeze before smiling at him.

There was a pause since Cody didn't say anything. They sat still, hand in hand as they got lost in their own thoughts.

"And if you're not comfortable with that option I'll look for a place for myself and you can move in with me then," Quinn said, continuing the conversation. He squeezed Cody's hand. "I'll sneak you into my house in my backpack if I have to," Quinn said, making Cody laugh before covering his mouth with his free hand.

"What's funny?" Quinn asked, grinning as he rested his head on Cody's shoulder. "I really would, you know."

The stairway became silent again, and the two boys just held hands and looked out into the streets.

"How do you stay so optimistic?" Cody asked, turning a bit before running his fingers through Quinn's curly dark hair. "You're always so sure that things will be alright."

"I don't know. I just am?" Quinn said, looking up at Cody he was glancing down at him. The boy had long lashes, and his face was free of bruises today.

Cody chuckled, pinching his boyfriend's cheek. "That's not an answer." He insisted but didn't prob Quinn for a better one.

The two stayed like that for a while, and their conversation drifts to comics and Quinn's family. Cody looked down at his boyfriend who was resting on him, and soon Quinn raised his head before smiling at Cody.

"Can I kiss you?" Quinn asked as his eyes lingered on Cody's pink lips for a bit too long.

Cody felt his face warm-up, but he sucked in his embarrassment in and nodded. "Y-yes," he stuttered, watching Quinn chuckle before reaching out to hold his face.

"You're so adorable," Quinn whispered when he rested his forehead on Cody's. He rubbed the boy's cheek with the base of his thumb before leaning in to connect their lips. He pressed up against the boy groaning when their tongues touched.

After a while Quinn pulled away from the kiss, smiling at Cody's now red face as he hummed to himself.

"I just want to kiss you all day, you know?" Quinn confessed, making Cody chuckled a bit before focusing his gaze on the bottom stair. The stairs were made of plain concrete that no one had bothered to paint over or level with some other material like wood.

Cody felt his heart rate increase and his lips tremble as he thought of what to say. "I like you too. Like a lot," he managed to get out in a breathy voice, emphasizing the last word. Sure, Quinn liked him, but Cody sometimes wondered if it was even possible to like someone as much as he liked Quinn. Did Quinn like him as much as Cody adored him?

"I like to kiss you too, like a lot," Cody muttered under his breath as he was reminded of pleasurable dreams when half the time was him just kissing Quinn a lot.

"That's nice to hear," Quinn said, looking at Cody with a slight smile on his face.

Quinn tapped Cody's shoulder, making the boy look up at him.

Cody frowned a bit. "What—?" he couldn't finish his sentence since Quinn took his face in his hands before planting a kiss on his mouth. Cody sighed into the kiss, reaching out to touch Quinn's face too. He moaned at the feeling of Quinn sucking on his tongue. He could feel his stomach twist up and his legs shake as Quinn deepened the kiss.

"Hey," Quinn let out, pulling away from the kiss. He rested his forehead against Cody's, staring into the boy's brown eyes. "Can I try something?" he asked, and Cody licked his lips, wondering what it was.

"What?" Cody asked, and Quinn's eyes fluttered to the front of the smaller boy's chest.

"Well, I was reading the other day and it said it feels good if you kiss there too," Quinn muttered. He already touched Cody's chest a lot, but he had been curious.

Cody looked down at the concrete stair beneath them. "Isn't that too much to do in public?" he muttered. He felt excited, but he wanted to offer a bit of common sense before jumping in.

"We're behind the shack..." Quinn trailed. "You won't take off your shirt, you'll just hold it up," Quinn offered, and Cody nodded, making the boy smile. Quinn reached under Cody's shirt, running his hands up his stomach like he usually did. He let his fingers brush his nipples, and Cody closed his eyes as always.

"You have to hold this up for me," Quinn explained, taking Cody's hands in his before pressing them on the boy's shirt. Cody nodded, pulling his shirt up until his whole chest was exposed. There they were, two brown buds already wrinkled from excitement.

"You know, this was less embarrassing in my head..." Quinn trailed, and Cody chuckled, feeling his face warm up. Quinn manned up, bending his head until his breath was fanning Cody's chest. He kissed one of the boy's nipples, twisting the other between his finger as he made to lick and suckle on the other.

Cody squirmed, tightening his hold on the fabric of his shirt as Quinn got bolder with his sucking. Cody let his shirt slip from his hands, but let his fingers bury themselves in Quinn's hair.

When the taller boy pulled away his eyes were pooling with an emotion that made Cody's legs shake. "Quinn..." he trailed, thinking of something.

"Hmm?" The older boy sat up straight, letting Cody's shirt fall back down.

"Maybe we should get stuff like condoms when we're heading home... for later?" Cody's voice grew smaller with every word, but Quinn picked them up. The taller boy's face warmed up, but he nodded, wrapping his hands around Cody before pulling him close.

"Sure," he muttered, kissing Cody's hairline. "Do you want to be on the top or bottom?" Quinn asked in a small voice after a while.

Cody's eyes widened a bit at the question. "Bottom," he muttered, and Quinn nodded into his hair. Cody had just assumed that Quinn had picked that up over time. He liked being touched and hovered over.

The thought of Quinn buried inside him as he moaned saying how good and tight, he felt made Cody's skin shiver with pleasure. His fantasies usually followed two paths—one where Quinn was inside him and couldn't shut up about how good he felt, and another where he would suck on Quinn for a long time, and then Quinn would then move his hips, thrusting into Cody's mouth. He would apologize somewhere along the line for getting the boy's face stained with cum because he couldn't hold it in.

Nonetheless, both involved Quinn really being into Cody so much that he couldn't hold himself.

Cody had a need to be wanted like that.

"What are you thinking about?" Quinn asked, making Cody blink. Cody could feel his face warm up.

"Nothing," he muttered as Quinn pulled away to look at him with a raised bow. He wondered if Quinn thought of stuff like that too, but he was too afraid to ask, feeling that reading magazines filled with pictures and erotica geared at older gay men did fuck with his fantasies a bit, meaning they possibly weren't normal teen ones.

The taller boy let Cody's none answer go and pressed a kiss to the boy's lips. The two kissed and held on to each other until the sun completely set. Cody's face still felt warm even when the two boys got up from the stairs and made to walk home together. They shared a kiss at the junction of Cody's street, and Quinn left right after with Cody waving him off.

CHAPTER TWENTY-TWO

- -

Quinn is standing by the front door of Cody's home. Quinn is side-stepping on the porch, humming as he makes to knock on the door. It was early un an afternoon, and there was a faint bark somewhere in the distance, while the birds in the tree at the backyard of Cody's flat made noise as they jumped from branch to branch.

Quinn frowned, knocking on the door again when he didn't get an answer. He knew someone was home. He had checked with their neighbors first.

Quinn's brows shot up when he heard someone shuffling on the other end. "Hello?" he calls when no one opens the door for him even then.

Quinn's mother had sent him out to bring Cody over for lunch. Cody didn't have a phone, so Quinn couldn't call him and ask, so he had to walk all the way to Cody's house instead. It was alright. Quinn knew Cody was always up to eat at his place, so it wasn't as if the boy would say no.

Quinn's frown deepened. No one replied. He presses his ear against the door. "Hello? Is anyone home?"

Quinn steps back from the door when it suddenly flies open, revealing a dark-haired man with a glare on his face. Quinn looked away, wondering why the boy seemed so angry.

"What do you want?" the young man asked, and Quinn winced at the smell of alcohol that came out from his mouth.

Quinn ran his fingers through his hair before speaking up. "I'm looking for Cody—"

"Why would you want to have anything to do with him?" The man asked, cutting Quinn off. Quinn sensed the passive aggressiveness in his voice. He also noticed how red the boy's eye whites were—he might have been high on something aside from drinking.

"I'm not sure how to answer that. I want to hang out with him, why does that concern you?" Quinn asked, getting more irritated by the minute.

Quinn could see the man's frown become deeper, and he noticed how his hands became fists beside him as his grit his teeth, but Quinn stood his ground, staring right back at him with an equally irritated gaze.

"You're the one he's fucking, aren't you?" the young man said out of nowhere. Quinn's eyes went wide as he clenched his jaw. He wondered what the older lad thought he was doing.

"Excuse me?" he asked, frowning. irritation stained his tone, and he was at his wit's end with the older boy. Quinn remembered that Cody only lived with his mother and brother, and if his hunch was correct this must the Charles that gave Cody bruises and wounds. Quinn felt the pitch of his stomach twist. He wanted to reach out and give Charles a tenth of what he frequently gave to Cody.

The young man seemed pleased with Quinn's reaction. "Don't lie to me. You're sleeping with him, aren't you? Disgusting fag." His voice was laced with venom. He was looking to offend and cut through thick skin.

Quinn knew that the boy was trying to get a reaction out of him. When he started dating Cody, he knew that antagonism and slurs would become a given someday but hearing a word like that directed at him had still shocked him. "I'm not—well, not yet. I'm dating him though. Is that a problem?" Quinn said, remaining calm. As much as it sucked to take in insults, he had read that not being emotional around people that sought you out to bully would help in the long run.

It worked. The boy's face seemed to grow warm at Quinn's answer. He hadn't been expecting Quinn to just shrug things off like that, and the boy didn't have much of anything left to say.

Quinn's eyes peered over the young man's shoulder. He needed to know if Cody was home. There was no need to verbally fight with Charles if Cody wasn't even around in the first place. His eyes went wide when he spotted the head of dark hair behind the young man.

"Cody!" Quinn yelled, spotting the smaller boy cowering behind Charles who was blocking the entrance to the house with his bulky frame. It seemed that Cody had shown up somewhere in the middle of their row with each other, and neither of them hand noticed. Cody seemed shocked at Quinn had called him, but he managed to smile at him from behind his brother.

"Fucking fags," Charles said, making Quinn's eyes focus on him again. There was a rage in his eyes, and Quinn could see from the way the expression in his eyes kept changing that he was trying to gauge if continuing the fight was worth it. Sure, he was bigger, but that also meant he would be slower and likely to tumble. Quinn played sports and was toned and in shape. Charles made his decision by stepping away from the door, creating space that Cody could use to leave the house.

"What are you waiting for? Get out before I change my mind," Charles said, making Cody hurry his steps. The smaller boy winced at the sound of the door being banged close behind him. Charles must have been pissed beyond words. Cody saw Quinn hadn't been taking his nonsense and entertaining him.

The porch became silent after the door had slammed close. Quinn and Cody stared at each other, not saying anything as they both recovered from what had just happened.

Quinn went to lean on the railing, and he held on the hot metal with his hands as he looked over at Cody who was hugging himself. "My mum asked if you'd like to come for dinner," Quinn said, breaking the silence.

"Oh," Cody chuckled a bit, rubbing the back of his neck. He was wearing a plaid top over faded jeans. "It's not like I can say no," he shrugged, looking at the door.

Quinn figured, but the joke had made him uncomfortable. He was used to just playing along with Cody and pretending that the bruises and wounds weren't there and pretending not to hear how badly he got yelled when he would wait for him to get inside his house before leaving. The two stood in silence, both of their minds swimming with thoughts they weren't sure they should vocalize or not. Quinn looked down at his sneakers. They didn't get as dirty anymore because it had been raining less over the past few weeks.

"That's your bother?" Quinn asked, breaking the silence. He leaned off the railings before walking over to Cody. He narrowed his eyes at the boy, reaching to hold Cody's chin before lifting the boy's face for inspection. There were no new bruises, and Quinn was glad because if there had been, he might have just knocked on the door again to have a word or two with the older lad.

"Yes, he is," Cody muttered, letting Quinn take his hand and pull him along with him so that the two boys stepped down the stairs together.

Quinn frowned. "That's really him, isn't it?" Quinn didn't think the two looked alike at all. The boy was huge, and had a pinkish tint to his skin, while Cody was ghostly and small. Or maybe it was a nutrition issue like his mother had suggested? Quinn wasn't quite sure.

"Half-brother. He's my half-brother," Cody clarified, sensing Quinn's confusion. Charle's mother had been their father's wife, and Cody's mother had been his mistress on his side. At a point, their father had decided he want to be with Cody's mum, and that's where a lot of the bitterness Charles felt for him came from.

"Oh, that makes sense," Quinn said, nodding at Cody's explanation before squeezing the boy's hand. He could sense that Cody didn't want to talk about it, so he controlled the urge hand to ask questions. The two walked in silence for a bit.

Quinn nibbled on his bottom lip, looking for what to talk about. "My mum made pork chops, and mashed potatoes. I knew you'd like some and that's why I came to call you—to eat lunch. I'm sorry if I might have caused any problems with your bother," Quinn rambled, realizing that he might have made Charles angry enough to act out on Cody when he went out.

Cody smiled, squeezing Quinn's hand. "It's okay. Thanks, really. I haven't eaten lunch," he said, looking over at Quinn.

Quinn mirrored the smile on the smaller boy's face as they both continued to walk towards his apartment complex. "That's good. I mean, it's not that you're hungry, but it's good that you want to eat... Am I making sense?"

Quinn asked, feeling his face warm up. He didn't know why he was a rambling mess this afternoon.

There was also a show Quinn wanted to watch with Cody on his phone—an indie movie about boys just like then. Quinn was a little embarrassed to ask but googling and trying to learn about himself so that he could be the best partner to Cody led him to discover a lot of gay media. Quinn was brought out of his thoughts when Cody laughed. He looked over at him, noticing the wide smile on the smaller boy's face.

The smile on Cody's face almost looked painful. It was wide and reached his eyes. There was something about Quinn's rambling that endeared him. Maybe it was how he panicked when he felt he had said something wrong, or how small his voice would get as he tried to straighten out what he had said.

Cody used to feel exhausted after smiling because he didn't do it very often, but now he smiled with ease around Quinn and his family, and dare he say he enjoyed it too.

The two eventually hold hands after a period of their fingers brushing as they walked side by side. Cody was a bit worried about his brother, but he didn't want to worry Quinn with his troubles—he himself personally didn't want to remember they existed, so he thought about the present, about heading home with Quinn to eat pork and mashed potatoes.

CHAPTER TWENTY-THREE

It's one of those days Cody insisted on sleeping at home. Quinn had walked Cody home, and the two boys were now in front of Cody's place. The neighborhood was quiet, except for the sound of birds in the distance. Charles' motorcycle was parked outside, and it made Cody nervous, but he didn't want to sleep over at Quinn's every night.

"I'll be fine," Cody muttered when Quinn asked him if he would be okay. For a minute Quinn wanted to suggest that he would sleep over at Cody's place, but he hadn't informed his mum and had left his phone at home.

"Okay," Quinn said after some hesitant. He let go of Cody's hand, and the two boys talked for a bit before Cody had to say goodbye to Quinn.

"I have to go," he said, realizing that they had been standing in front of the flat for at least thirty minutes. Quinn gave him a smile, but it was forced. He didn't want to let Cody go, and Cody didn't want to go, but he had to.

"Okay, by," Quinn said, making to walk away. He paused, running back to Cody before pulling him into a tight hug. "But after this," Quinn said, pulling away before holding on to Cody's face and giving the boy a kiss.

Quinn let go of Cody, and he waved goodbye before turning away and leaving for real this time. Cody watched the taller boy walk into the street and disappear into the night. It was late in the evening now, and only a few streetlights were on since most of them had burnt out.

Cody's smile falls when he turned and stared at the door to his home. I reached out to open it but found out it was locked. Anxiety filled him when he realized he would have to knock. He didn't want to, knowing who would open it up.

Cody hugged himself, biting on his lower lip as he stared at his door. His eyes had glossed over with tears, knowing that his brother was the one that was going to end up opening the door. He reached to rap a few knocks on the door, wondering if he'd be able to get out of being hit today—but that was a layman's dream.

He waited for a bit, and when the wait hit five minutes, he felt that Charles maybe wanted him to sleep outside. He was already turning and making to head down the stairs when the door flew open. He froze in shock, turning to look over at Charles.

"Oh, you're back. I thought you were staying over at his place," the bigger boy said, leaning on the door frame with his weight. Cody opened his mouth but closed it. He wanted to ask if Charles had seen them talking together a while back, but he didn't want to have that conversation with Charles, knowing where it would head.

"You're a leech, that's what you are. You hang on to anything that will take care of you," Charles spat when Cody didn't react to his first sentence. The smaller boy still didn't say anything this time, and it was starting to piss Charles off.

Charles' blood started to boil. "Why aren't you saying anything. Talk. Say something. Don't just stand there and act like you're being victimized—"

"I don't have anything to say," Cody said, cutting his brother off. He hated the line of Charles claiming he was 'acting' like was victimized. Charles beat him up any chance he could. How could he act like he was being mistreated if it was nothing but the truth?

Charles was taken aback by the coldness in Cody's tone. Often times the boy's voice would shake like he was close to tears, but today he just seemed exhausted. Very exhausted. Charles rose a brow at Cody's words, staring down at the smaller boy with cold eyes. "Ah, I see. It's that boy that's making you feel like hot shit. What's his name?" Charles asked, making Cody's worst fears come through. He didn't want Quinn to have anything to do with Charles. Quinn didn't deserve to be involved with his terrible brother just because was dating him.

His lips turned down, and he let out a sigh. It was too late. Charles would figure out his name or seek him out because he was obsessed with having a hand in Cody's life. "Q-Quinn," Cody managed to say, hoping that telling him would be enough to convince Charles to leave him alone. He smiled a bit, remembering Quinn telling him that his full name was Quincey when they were laying on his bed together one night. That was their secret. He claimed that Kyle was the only other person in their grade that knew.

"Hmm, okay," Charles said, searching his head for what to say. He had expected Cody to try and hide the boy's name, and that would have given him a reason to pester him, but Cody wasn't biting tonight. The smaller boy was already exhausted from the conversation. Charles had a habit of jumping around and not really saying anything that he wanted to really say. He just wanted to agitate his stepbrother so that he could have a reason to bother him. Cody was just tired. He needed to sleep. He wondered if Charles would even let him into the room, they both supposedly shared.

Charles let out a grunt. "Does he know what you've done?"

Cody frowned looking up at Charles. "Does he know I've done what?" Cody asked, feeling his chest squeeze up.

Charles grinned before chuckling. He was glad to have finally received a reaction from Cody. "Does he know you killed my father—your father? Does he know that?" Charles asked, making Cody square his shoulders. The smaller boy looked at the floor, deciding that he didn't want to answer that.

Charles rattled on and on about the incident that Cody was tired to even try and defend himself. Charles needed someone to blame for his father's death, and Cody was an easy target.

"So, he doesn't?" Charles said, trying to pick on Cody's nerves. Cody remained silent.

"I might tell him—just for his own good. He needs to know what he's getting into," Charles said. Cody shook his head before looking up at Charles with a frown.

Cody groaned. "You're going to lie to him—"

Charles cut Cody off before he could finish his sentence. "They're not lies," the larger boy insisted. This is how it always went down. Charles would blame Cody, and Cody would defend himself, and Charles would hit Cody and force him to say it was his fault.

The two boys stated at each other since Cody didn't say anything in response. After a while, Cody looked away, ending the staring contest. He tried to brush past Charles to get into the house, but the older boy blocked hid path.

"Excuse me," Cody muttered. His voice was low, and he seemed exhausted. Charles must have picked up that it wasn't the best time to bother him because he stepped away from the door like he was asked it.

Cody sighed in relief, thankful for the fact that Charles didn't decide to start a fight with him.

As Cody walked into the house Charles said, "You don't deserve to be happy."

Cody ignored the boy, making a beeline to the hallway so that he could get into their room. When he shut the room door behind him, he also heard the front door slam closed. Cody's lips trembled as he slid to the floor.

Although Cody wanted to ignore Charles' words, he couldn't help but replay them in his mind as he stared at the bedroom wall. He'd believed those words once upon a time, but not anymore. He wanted to be happy, He wanted to live, and not just exist.

He closed his eyes, taking a deep breath. "I deserve to be happy," Cody muttered under his breath before opening his eyes again and getting up. He spread a bedsheet on the beside the bed Charles' stayed on, before laying down and curling up into fetal position. The floor was heard, and under Charles' bed smelled bad. He felt more comfortable in Quinn's bed.

He closed his eyes, repeating the words from before. "I deserve to be happy." Hearing the words from his own mouth made him feel stronger. A smile formed on his face, and he soon closed his eyes, deciding to sleep.

CHAPTER TWENTY-FOUR

The kitchen area of Quinn's home was quiet and filled the aromas of spices. Quinn was sitting by the kitchen island while his mother worked on preparing fish. It was late in the afternoon, and the sun was pouring into the small kitchen/living room through the open window. Quinn's mother had opened it to try and get some of the fish smell out of the apartment.

Earlier in the day, Quinn had spent some time in Karl's apartment. The two boys had talked when Karl suddenly brought up Cody.

"So, how is he?" Karl had asked, making Quinn look up from his deck of cards. They were squashed behind the sofa, playing cards in secret so Karl's eleven-year-old brother wouldn't bug them and ask to join.

"Who, Cody?" Quinn had asked, and Karl had nodded. "Well, he's doing alright. We couldn't hang out today because he had a pile of homework to go through since he didn't go to school for a while," Quinn had said, and Karl had hummed, watching as Quinn played a move and made him pick some cards from the deck.

"That's good to hear, but I was asking about something else," Karl had muttered, making Quinn raise a brow at his friends.

"What's something else?" Quinn had asked, getting curious from how red his friend's face was turning.

Karl shrugged. "Well, I was wondering if it was weird with a boy. Like, what is Cody like when it comes to that stuff? All the kissing and touching must be weird if you know what I mean..." Karl had trailed, and Quinn's face had grown warm. "Also, sex. I think the sex would be kind of weird too," Karl had added.

"It's not weird. I like it a lot," Quinn had said. "But then again, I'm not sure if I'm the person you should ask this since I've never done anything with a girl," Quinn had added and Karl had nodded.

"You know. I should have realized something was off sooner, considering the hottest boy in our school hadn't kissed a girl ever at age eighteen," Karl had said, and Quinn had rolled his eyes, chuckling under his breath.

He stared at his friend, locking eyes with Karl. "We haven't done it though," he had said, looking down at his hands. "Gone all the way, that is," Quinn had said, nibbling on his bottom lip.

"I'm sure it'll be alright," Karl had said, and Quinn had looked up at his friend. It was strange. Karl had just called gay stuff weird, but he was also being nice about the two boys being together. It didn't matter, Quinn thought. His friend was doing his best.

The sound of a passing car brought Quinn out of his thoughts. Quinn groaned, raising his head from the counter. Quinn was bored out of his mind now. He kicked his leg, looking at the back of his mother's head. Cody's brother doesn't look like him at all—

"I hope you didn't probe him about it?" Quinn's mother said, cutting her son off. She really hoped he hadn't been that rude for no reason.

"I didn't really," Quinn said, wrapping his hands around the mug of hot chocolate that he'd gotten for himself. "It just made me kind of curious," Quinn said, looking down at the swirl of milk and cocoa.

"Good, don't be invasive. He might be your boyfriend, but there's a line, and you shouldn't cross it," Quinn's mother advised him. Raising up a finger to the roof. "Do you understand?"

Quinn sighed, "I understand."

"There's a likelihood that that's not his brother at all, or for the most part, just his half-brother. I told you about family issues. Problems are common in that kind of setting. Cody's lucky to have you. It can be damaging for a kid, but I'm sure he'll be leaving his home at the end of the school year, won't he?" Quinn's mother said. His mother had hit the nail right on the head. Charles was Cody's half-brother, and Cody had told him so.

Quinn nodded his head before resting it on the marble surface of the kitchen island.

"I talked to his brother..." Quinn trailed. His voice had been small, but his mother had picked it up.

Quinn's mother paused turning the stew in the pot in front of her to turn to her son. "You talked to him about what?"

Quinn shrugged. "Nothing really." He narrowed his eyes at the wall. "He just seemed really—bitter?"

Quinn's mother looks over at her son, nodding her head. "Yes, it does sound like family issues." She concluded that she had been right before turning back to the food in front of her.

Partial silence soon took reign in the kitchen. Quinn just watched his mother work. She moved about, dipping pieces of fish into a frying pan before returning to the stew she was making. Quinn watched them sizzle in the oil, sometimes bubbles of oil would jump from the pan and hit his mother's arm, making her winch.

Janet walked into the kitchen/living room. She made to greet her mum before ruffling her brother's hair.

"Where are you going?" Quinn asked, pushing her hand away.

"I'm going to work. I'm trying to make some extra money so I can get a friend a gift on her birthday," she said, and Quinn hummed, watching as his sister waltzed over to his mother before peering over her shoulder.

"Can I have some fish?" she asked. Her mother rolled her eyes, but let the girl pick a piece from the plate of fried fish. Janet grinned, moving to sit beside Quinn on the kitchen island.

"Quinn, invite Cody over next week. I rented a new movie," Janet said, biting into the piece of fish in her hand. "It's a good Spanish drama," she said, and Quinn rolled his eyes.

"Whatever," he said, smiling a bit. Though Quinn was being a bit rude, he was quite happy that Cody and his sister were getting along. The smaller boy had started to talk around her, and who knew all that was needed was a good Spanish drama series that they both liked.

"When's dad coming back today?" Janet asked their mum. Quinn shivered a bit, still feeling strange about how his dad had reacted to the news that he was dating Cody. It seemed like his old man was avoiding him, and Quinn felt uncomfortable about it.

"He said he'd be back late this evening," Quinn's mum said. Her voice was flat, and it showed that she knew what Quinn was thinking and feeling.

"Janet, aren't you going to be late for work?" she asked, trying to get Janet to hurry up and leave so that she could have alone time to talk to Quinn.

The girl raised her hands up in surrender, getting off the kitchen stool before walking out of the apartment and shutting the door. That left Quinn and his mother alone again by themselves. The kitchen was silent for a while, only being tinted by the sound of Quinn's mother running the tap from time to time. She started humming a song, and Quinn joined her.

Quinn's mother stopped humming. "That reminds me, what do you plan to do after graduation?" Quinn's mother asked, turning to look at her son.

Quinn shrugged. "I was thinking about checking some mechanic shops for an apprenticeship, that's what Karl's doing." Quinn's mother hummed, nodding her head.

"What about Cody? What does he want to do when he graduates? I'm sure college is out of the option like most people around here," she asked as she stirred the pot of stew in front of her before throwing in diced onions.

"I don't know," he muttered, running his finger through his hair. "He doesn't want to tell me things. I mean, it's okay. He doesn't have to tell me everything, but sometimes it feels like he's afraid of my reaction or he just doesn't want to bother me with it—"

"He'll tell you at the right time. Be patient, and just be there for him as much as you can now," Quinn's mother said, cutting him off. She placed the cover of pot over it, letting the stew steam on its own before turning to Quinn.

Quinn sighed before shrugging his shoulder. "It's just," he paused, looking down at the tiled floor as he tried to think of what to say. "I want to help. I know you're right—"

"I'm always right," Quinn's mother said, making the boy's head shot up. He saw his mother grinning at him, and a part of him was annoyed, but he also wanted to laugh.

Quinn grunted. "Wow, such humility." His voice was steaming with sarcasm, but his mother ignored it, nodding her head and fanning her face with her hand. They both started to laugh, and Quinn hummed when his mother approached him to hug. She smelt like fish, oil, and spices, but Quinn didn't think he'd rather have it any other way. Being with Cody had taught him the little things in life he often took for granted were precious. Things like a loving family—a mother you could talk to.

CHAPTER TWENTY-FIVE

I t was evening, and the roosters outside were cooing. The roads were relatively quiet. Which was quite a contrast to earlier in the afternoon yesterday when late teens in blue caps and grows gathered with their parents or talked to each other. It was the end of the school year, and it had felt weird for Cody to wake up without the pit of dread in his stomach that formed when he remembered he still had homework and essays to have due. All of that was over now. He'd graduated just yesterday. No one had come to the ceremony with him, but Quinn's parents had gotten him food and invited him to spend the night.

In the morning, he stayed clear from Charles, waiting for the young man to leave for the day before he started planning his departure. When the clock hit three in the afternoon, he went to the room he shared with Charles. He took out his small black rucksack before he started packing up the little belongings he owned, into it. Sometimes he would stop to go through everything, hoping that he wasn't leaving anything behind.

The fact that high school was over had only started to seem real today because he was moving out of his house. It was early in the evening, and he was squinting under the red light of the only bulb in the room as he tried to get his things from under the bed.

Charles got to use the cupboard to keep his things, while Cody had to stuff his in nook and crannies where Charles wouldn't be angry when he saw them. Having things scattered behind drawers, under the bed and tucked somewhere above the shelves made it hard to get his things together, but he eventually did.

Cody looked around the room one last time, hoping he didn't forget anything. "I think that's about it," he whispered under his breath, smiling to himself as he zipped up the backpack he was holding in his hands.

A grin broke on his lips as he realized what was happening. He was saying goodbye to the cold floor, goodbye to the cigarette smoke, and goodbye to Charles' yelling and alcohol use.

He was really leaving.

Cody was planning to head over to Quinn's place. Quinn's parents had pulled him aside a week ago to tell him it was okay to stay at their place. When he had been leaning on refusing, they had told him to think of it as a holiday. He could simply stay until he figured things out if he wanted. He had given in. He did need a place to stay, and nothing felt more right than being with Quinn. His face heated up at the mere thought of waking up beside Quinn every morning. They would shower together, watch movies with his sisters, and touch each other when everyone else was away.

Cody's smile widened as he looked out into the room. "I'm going to leave this place," he said, letting out a small laugh. It's one of relief and happiness. His feet felt light, and so did his chest. He couldn't wait to get away from Charles. It was as if years of abuse were finally being unraveled in his head as he acknowledged how terrible things had been for him. Getting kicked, slapped, punched and hurt in general. He couldn't believe he had dealt with all that for years.

He hummed, bending a bit to see if he had left anything under Charles' bed. One last look wouldn't harm him, he felt. He stood up straight when he heard the door creak open behind him. He turned to find Charles by the door giving him a frown.

"What are you doing?" the older boy asked, Cody had been gone yesterday, and Cody hadn't informed Charles or his mother about his plans. He didn't feel like he had needed too. Charles wanted him gone anyway, and Charles' mother never wanted to talk to Quinn.

Cody tensed up, letting out a sigh before he made to sit on the floor. He looked over at Charles again, nibbling his bottom lip before answering the boy's question. "I'm packing my things," he announced, tightening his grip on his washed-out backpack.

Charles rose a brow at him, walking over to him before taking a sit on the only bed in the room. The mattress sunk with his weight, and the bed frame creaked a bit as Charles adjusted his sitting position. The bed was twin-sized, and Charles had outgrown it years ago. Cody didn't have a bed of his own. He slept on the floor with the roaches and dust.

"Why? Where are you going? You have nowhere to go," Charles said, making Cody's lip draw into a thin line. To think with that information Charles had been the person to threaten him to leave the house.

Cody bit down on his lower lip, strapping on his bag before getting up from the tiled floor. "I'm leaving," he said, staring directly at Charles. He wasn't going to answer the boy's question from before. It wasn't his business where Cody went.

Cody was wearing faded black jeans, and one of his many cheap graphic t-shirts. A lot of his clothes were already at Quinn's place. He just had to pick up after himself at home.

The room was silent for a while when Charles didn't say anything in reply. The two boys watched each other with unmoving gazes—Cody's lighter brown ones staring into Charles' dark ones. Cody had his brows knitted into a frown, and he was putting up a brave face, but his hands were shaking, and deep down he was scared. You didn't overcome the fear of your bully overnight, and Charles could hurt him right now. Cody's eyes dart to the door, as he thought of leaving. Charles gets up from the bed, before walking to block the boy's way.

"You're leaving," Charles said, smirking. "Is that so?" The older boy laughed before his features came together to form a cold look.

"You're not going anywhere," he said. His voice made a chill run up Cody's spine, but the small boy still attempted to walk past Charles. He gets shoved back, making him stumble a bit before finding his feet.

"What is your problem? You wanted me to leave after graduation, and that's what I'm doing, let me go!" Cody couldn't help yelling. His blood was boiling, and he was on the verge of shedding hot tears.

"You want me to let you go so that you can meet that Quinn boy? Not a chance," Charles said, reaching out to gran and twist Cody's hand.

"You don't deserve happiness. You're a piece of shit. I'm not letting you leave to be better off while my mother and I rot here because of you—because of your mother," the older boy drags Cody out of the room by the arm before stuffing him into the small bathroom at the end of the hallway. Cody's eyes went wide when he noticed what was happening.

"My mother is working all night today, so scream as much as you want, no one's going to hear your voice," Charles said, blocking the bathroom door.

The flickering orange light sparks from time to time, filling the silence void of the boys' voices.

Cody opened his mouth, wanting to speak. "Why—"

"Shut up," Charles said, cutting Cody off before he could finish. He looked down at Cody who was now sitting on the browning tiles before turning and shutting the door behind him.

Cody felt his heart all. He stared at the door until his eyes get blurred with unshed tears.

The boy could hardly breathe. He looks down at the floor, reaching up to cover his face with his hands before he beings to sob.

Will Quinn worry about me? He wondered, trying to control his tears.

Cody was losing hope very fast. Even if Quinn worried and came over, he wondered if Charles would let him in. Cody wondered if Charles would lie about his whereabouts, or tell Quinn lies about their father's death. Cody didn't know.

"God damn it!" he screams, pulling his hair until his scalp began to burn from pain. He needed any sensation—anything to numb out the despair building in his chest.

Cody felt the tears make their way down his cheeks. He sits up by the tiled wall, looking up at the leaking sink. His vision blurred again, and his throat felt coarse from his sobs.

He hoped Quinn would come and find him.

CHAPTER TWENTY-SIX

Cody was still in the small bathroom shared by him, Charles, and Charles' mother. It was quiet aside from the dripping noise from the leaking sink. He was sitting by the door now, and he had his face buried in his hands as he sobbed in silence. He had been locked in the bathroom for the past two hours, and he was starting to feel the effects of being enclosed in the small smelly space.

"Cody run, now!"

He squirmed, remembering what his father told him as he pushed him out of the door. The man had stroked his hair before looking back at the house.

"I'm going to get your mother."

Those were the man's last words. He had said before he disappeared back into the burning build. He never came out. Cody's mum and dad didn't survive. The roof had sunken in and crashed while Cody's dad had been trying to get his mum out of the flames.

Cody had remembered standing by the road and watching the house burn down as he waited for firemen to come. They had been too late, and one of the neighbor's had shuffled him out of the tragedy sight before calling his father's ex-wife to get him.

He had been ten years old then. It had been eight years since his parents died, and Charles would not let it go.

Cody groaned, feeling his side sting with pain when he moved a bit. His eyes would flutter close sometimes, and he would take a nap for a minute or two to counter the effects of his crying on him. A pounding headache from the sobbing and hair-pulling was starting to create pressure in his skull. Cody couldn't think. It was too painful to think. He was having one of these brief naps when he heard someone pounding on the door.

How long had it been since Charles had thrown him into the bathroom? He didn't know. He'd been knocked out for a bit. When he had gotten here there was dim light coming through the small window at the top, but now it was nothing, but pitch darkness cast away by the faulty light bulb. The knocking was getting louder with every bang. The knocking didn't stop, and Cody could hear Charles groan in the distance.

His eyes peeled open again, and hope soon filled him, and he was soon kneeling by the bathroom door with his ear pressed against the wooden door.

The knocking grew louder, and Cody felt whoever it was must have been at the door for at least thirty minutes. Cody's breath hiked when he heard footsteps in the hallway. Charles must have been going to see who was at the door.

Cody could feel his heart beating against his ribcage as he strained his ears to listen in. He could hear Charles opening the door, and he tried to steady his breathing since he had an idea who was behind it.

The voices in the distance were muffled but Cody could still heat them. It was one of the few times he was glad for the paper-thin walls in their house.

Charles groaned. "Oh, it's you again."

Cody's eyes widened in interest. "Who? Quinn?" he muttered under his breath, hoping that it was his boyfriend that had come for him.

And soon enough Cody heard Quinn's smooth voice respond to Charles' words.

"Yes, it's me again," Quinn said. "Where's Cody? He's supposed to have come over to my place. We're worried."

"He's not coming," Charles said, and Cody's heart fell. Imagining how his brother was possibly leaning by the door frame with his hands folded.

"What? Why not? We made plans for this since last week." Quinn's voice sounded rightly confused. There was no way Cody would say no now in favor of staying in a house infested by people he hated so much.

Cody's ears zoned out of the conversation, and Charles' and Quinn's bickering were no more than whispers he couldn't pick up. The beating of Cody's heart was making it hard to concentrate on the faint voices in the conversation.

Cody sighed before closing his eyes when their voices grew faint. "Come on..." he scolded himself, holding on to his forehead as he tried to force himself to focus. He tried again, placing his ear against the door at a position he hoped would let him hear better. A smile broke across his face. He could hear them in the distance again.

Charles was saying something now. "Has Cody ever mentioned our dad?" Cody could feel his heart sinking at those words. Charles was going to lie to Quinn. The older boy was going to pin something horrible on him.

"No, he hasn't. I was asking about Cody though, so why are you bringing that up?" Quinn asked.

Charles whistled before laughing. "You need to know something important," he said.

"No, don't..." Cody trailed under his breath as he closed his eyes. His whole body was beginning to tremble as his eyes clouded with unshed tears. He wondered why Charles was doing this. He wondered why Charles would be so cruel to try and cut him off from the one person that loved him.

Cody only felt more disturbed when he couldn't hear anything at all anymore. Charles must have taken Quinn out of the house—and hence, out of earshot. He could feel his heart racing, and he could feel sweat build up under his cotton shirt as he wondered how much Charles was telling Quinn—how many lies and manipulated facts he was adding to the already worn out accusation.

Cody sat on the bathroom floor again before pulling his knees to his chest. "Why?" he asked himself, giving up. His voice echoed in the room as the sink continued to leak in the background.

Cody coughed, sobbing. "What did I do to deserve this?" he asked himself, feeling his body shut down.

His eyes wandered to the drug cabinet just above the sink. His stepmother took a lot of aspirin. It was tempting to just get up and put one, two, three—multiple pills into his system and just give up the ghost. He didn't want to be here with Charles, and he didn't think he could go back to a time when he wasn't close to Quinn. His vision blurred, and he looked away from the cabinet. He was too tired to think of that now. What was the use? He was already walking corpse. He didn't know what living felt like. He'd just been existing.

Cody fidgets with his fingers as he waits, unsure of what was going on behind closed doors. He had stopped sobbing. He had no tears left to shed. His throat was dry, and he felt a bit dehydrated. His head was also pounding with pain.

Quinn wasn't an idiot. Cody didn't expect him to outright believe Charles, but your brain didn't work right when you were as exhausted, scared and worried as Cody was. Cody closes his eyes as he tries to push all the jumbling thoughts that were giving him anxiety to the back of his mind.

"Please hurry..." he muttered even though Quinn couldn't hear him, and with those words he escaped into his mind, hoping that everything would be alright.

CHAPTER TWENTY-SEVEN

- -

From the distance, the commotion on the patio of the Landgrab's bungalow was normal. Charles was known around the neighborhood for being brute with force and quick to anger, so the sight of him talking down to a dark-haired boy was not strange.

Quinn was standing on the top stair in his coat, trying to look past Charles' figure that was blocking the way into the house. It was a little past eight in the evening, and Quinn was starting to worry, seeing as Cody's brother was keen on trying to get him to listen to his rubbish.

"You need to know what he's done," the older boy insisted, blocking Quinn's path again.

Quinn raised his head. "I just need Cody to come out with me. He can tell me himself," he said, putting his hands into the pockets of his jacket to try to keep them warm. The weather was oddly cold that night, and Quinn wasn't appreciating the fact that he was standing out.

"I already told you, he's not going anywhere," Charles said, frowning as his grip on the two corners of the entrance tightened. He was using his whole body to block the path.

Quinn sighed as he looked down at the ground. His eyes were tired, and he was feeling less comfortable out in the cold.

"You don't care to know what he's done? He killed someone," Charles said, moving out of the way so that he was standing out in the cold with Quinn.

Charles closed the door behind him, before resting on it. "I just wanted to warn you. He's a walking curse. You don't need him," he said.

Charles was a bit worried by the confusion in Quinn's face. The boy didn't look shocked, just irritated. "Of course, he grew up to be a fag too. You're a good-looking lad why are you entertaining him? Does he do weird stuff to make up for being a dude?" Charles was saying whatever now—anything to make Cody lose his shot at happiness.

Quinn sighed, rolling his eyes. "Look, I don't care—"

"He killed our father," Charles injected, cutting him off.

Quinn groaned, shaking his head. "You're just making up stuff now, aren't you?" Cody was so small and prone to hurting himself. He couldn't even kill a rat.

Quinn felt exhausted. He had been bummed when his father had been a little cold and distant before warming up to him over the course of a few months, but Cody had it worse. Way wore than he could ever imagine. He couldn't believe that he had endured people that hated his very being for so long.

Cody deserved better.

"I'm not making stuff up," Charles insisted, pulling Quinn out of his thoughts. The young man's voice came out croaked. His voice was shaking. Quinn raised a brow when he noticed a shimmer in the young man's eyes.

"Are you—" Quinn paused, narrowing his eyes at Charles. "Are you crying?" he asked in a soft voice, both taken aback and worried.

The sight of the young man in front of him breaking down into tears threw Quinn off. He wasn't sure what to do so he just stood there, watching as Charles rubbed at his eyes with the base of his palms.

"He killed my father, and he gets to be happy." A dark look pooled in Charles' eyes. "Fuck, I hate his guts."

Quinn frowned. "Hey—"

"It's so unfair!" The young man said, cutting Quinn off before he could finish.

Quinn frowned a bit before his features relaxed. He watched Charles with a sympathetic look. He wasn't sure what to make of what was happening, so he stared at his feet instead.

"If my father hadn't gone to live with his mother and started a relationship with her, he'd still be alive—he wouldn't have been there during the fire. The fact that Cody's survived it is like his mother's ghost mocking my mother—me," the young man said, fighting sniffles as he looked up. A frown was still on his face as he tried to control his tears.

Quinn felt uncomfortable. He wasn't sure what to say to any of Charles' rambling, but at least he had a better picture of what was going on.

"I don't know what you're going through, but you can't possibly blame a kid for a fire that he didn't start?" Quinn said, and Charles didn't say anything to him.

"Hey, I know you lost your dad, and you're super sad about it..." Quinn trailed. "But he's Cody's dad too, you know?"

Charles remained silent, but Quinn kept talking. "How do you think Cody feels when you say stuff like he killed his own dad?" There was still no answer from Charles. "Your father did a bad thing. He married your mum and cheated on her and got another woman pregnant. his decision to chase the woman he got pregnant years later has nothing to do with Cody," Quinn continued.

"Your father died. I'm sure you're both sad, and looking for someone to blame it on help you cope, but how long are you going to grieve like this?" Quinn felt a little odd—a bit like his mother when she was giving him a lecture on life.

There was a pause where Charles was silent. A minute passed, and the young man spoke up. "He's in the bathroom."

Quinn looked up at Charles. "What?" He hadn't expected the young man to say anything.

"Cody. Cody's in the bathroom. I locked him up there, you should be able to find the key in the lock," Charles said, moving away from the front door. "Come on, go in before I change my mind," Charles said when Quinn didn't move an inch.

The dark-haired boy looked from Charles to the door before heading towards it. He reached out and turned the knob, and the door clicked open.

He smiled, relieved that it wasn't a prank before turning his head to face Cody. "Thank you," he said. He wasn't sure what had come over Cody's brother to get him to allow him in, but he was grateful.

Charles gritted his teeth, looking away from Quinn. "Go get him before I change my mind," he said, and Quinn did as he was told. He slipped into the living room and made a beeline to the hallway, searching for the bathroom door.

CHAPTER TWENTY-EIGHT

Quinn walked through the dark hallway, in search of the bathroom door. There were three doors. Two at each side, and one at the end. He headed straight down, guessing that was the door to the bathroom. They were positioned there in most houses. His heart sank when he heard sobbing, and as he got closer, he noticed the dangling keys still on the lock like Charles had said they would be.

"Cody? Cody is that you?" Quinn asked as his hands touched the cool wooden surface of the door. The crying got louder, and Quinn's stomach twisted. "It's Quinn. I'm here, please don't cry," Quinn said in a soothing voice, fumbling with the lock until it clicks open with a turn of the key.

"Cody... " Quinn trailed, not knowing what to make of the crying person curled up by the door. Cody was shaking and his hair stuck to his wet face.

"Cody..." Quinn said again, making to kneel by him before pushing away the wet strands of hair clinging to his face. The boy shook like he was shivering, and his eyes fluttered open before going wide.

"Quinn...?" the smaller boy let out in a surprised tone, letting his eyes take in Quinn's face.

Quinn smiled, moving to kneel beside him. "Yes, it's me."

Cody's lips turned up in an exhausted smile before he burst into another round of sobs.

Quinn sighed, pulling his boyfriend into a hug, letting him cry as he rubbed circles on his back. The boy's clothes were wet from sweat, but Quinn didn't mind. He couldn't imagine how long he'd been trapped here, and it made him enraged that Charles would ever think of doing this to his brother.

"I thought you'd hate me," Cody sighed into Quinn's chest. "Didn't Charles say something?"

"He did," Quinn confirmed.

Cody pulled away from Quinn before rubbing his eye with the base of his palms. "Thanks for not believing him." The boy sniffed.

"You'd think I'd believe him?" Quinn asked, frowning a bit. It was a joke, but he was a little hurt.

Cody opened his mouth before closing it, then opening his mouth to speak again. "No, I—I was just scared," he said, covering his face with his palms. "I don't know... I'm sorry."

Quinn pulled Cody back into a hug. "Don't say sorry. You've been saying sorry for things that aren't your fault all your life. Don't apologize."

Cody sighed, nodding into Quinn's shoulder.

After a while of just hugging each other in the bathroom, the two pulled away from each other.

Quinn smiled at Cody, squeezing his shoulders. "Where's your stuff?"

"In the room. I'll go get them," he said, getting up. He wobbled a bit but managed to walk out of the bathroom without tripping. Quinn got up too, following Cody out of the bathroom.

He paused walking when he spotted Charles looking at them from the edge of the hallway's entrance.

"Thanks again," Quinn managed, looking at Charles. The dark-haired young man looked pissed. He looked away, he seemed to be shocked by Quinn's thanks.

He folded his hands across his chest, letting out a grunt. "The both of you should just leave fast. Get out before I change my mind," he said, turning and walking into the living room. Quinn frowned but did as he was told. He went in the direction bedroom Cody shared with his brother.

Cody had already stepped out with his backpack when Quin reached the door. The smaller boy closed the door behind him, before letting Quinn take his hand in his.

"Oh, you're out. Is that all?" Quinn asked, noticing how small the backpack was. Aside from his schoolbooks, he guessed a few clothes were in it.

Cody shrugged, giving his boyfriend a small smile. "Yeah, I don't have much."

There was a period of silence. Quinn looked at Cody and noticed that the boy looked tired—so tired, but there was a smile on his pale face. His dark long hair looked like it had been messily brushed aside with fingers, which was probably the case.

Quinn smiled squeezing Cody's smaller hand. "Come on, let's leave. My mum will get worried. She made dinner for you and all, and you couldn't make it."

Cody hummed as Quinn led the way out of the hallway. Cody caught Charles looking at him from his seat on the sofa as the two boys slipped past the door and out of his house. When the cold breeze from the night weather slapped Cody's face, the boy let out a breath he'd been holding. He was finally freed from Charles. From the abuse. From everything.

The two boys walked through the dimly lit streets in the cold night, huddling together, hand in hand—and even if it was cold Cody's chest was burning with warmth. Quinn chattered on about every and anything, while Cody looked at him in awe. He couldn't express how grateful he was to Quinn and his family.

He felt free.

Alive.

It didn't take long for both of them to reach Quinn's apartment. Quinn and Cody were sitting by the Kitchen Island as they watched Quinn's mother warm up some food. The kitchen/living room was bathed in the warm orange light of fluorescent light bulbs. The rest of Quinn's family had gone to bed, leaving only the three of them awake. A slow drizzle had started outside, and the sound of raindrops hitting the glass windows resounded through the room.

Quinn's mother looked towards the kitchen window before resting her hands on her waist. "Ah, it's a good thing you two made it home before it started raining."

Quinn nodded, reaching out for Cody's hand before giving it a small squeeze. They'd dropped his bag off in Quinn's room before Quinn's mother had shooed them back into the kitchen for something to eat. "Yeah. It would have been terrible to be drenched in rain."

Cody hummed in agreement, smiling softly as he looks down at their conjoined hands. The boys were sitting on stools by the kitchen island.

The microwave beeped, and they all looked towards it. Quinn's mother takes a transparent container with a brown soup out of the microwave before pouring its contents into two different bowls. "Here," she said, passing a bowl to Cody and Quinn each.

The two boys started to eat when Quinn's mother gave them spoons from the cutlery cabinet. The woman stared at both of them, and an apologetic smile graced her face when she caught Cody's eyes. "How are you? I hope nothing bad happened. everyone was a little worried since you didn't come over sooner."

"Nothing bad happened," Cody insisted shaking his head as he took a spoon full of soup.

Quinn's mother knew that was a lie, but she didn't push. The boy would open up to her later. It could be a few weeks, months or even in the next few years, but she decided to wait. She folded her hands over the kitchen island instead as she leaned forward. "I hope so, feel free to make yourself at home. Quinn's happy to have you here."

Cody's eyes went wide before he turned to his boyfriend and finds him smiling.

Quinn shrugged. "It's true."

Quinn's mother laughed, watching as the smaller boy blushed before turning away. He was such a character, the lad.

The two boys talked to Quinn's mother as the rain got heavier. Cody was still amazed by how at ease Quinn was with his mum. He had picked up that the boy had problems with his father now after coming out, but he could tell they were getting better since Quinn and his mother were talking about the man.

"Your dad wants you to go and work for his friend. He gives good starting salaries to his apprentices," Quinn's mum said and Quinn nodded. He still looked a bit uncomfortable, the way he did whenever his father was brought up in the past few months, but he seemed a lot freer about it.

"I know, I talked to dad about that already," he said, and Quinn's mother smiled, nodding her head.

Some time by twelve in the night they both headed decided it was time to take a shower before heading to Quinn's room.

CHAPTER TWENTY-NINE

When the two boys were in Quinn's room Quinn walked over to the dresser to grab some clothes to change into.

Cody blushed and he looked away when Quinn starts to change. He cursed himself under his breath. He had watched the boy do it so many times, he wasn't sure why he was so nervous. He looks around, realizing that he was going to wake up in this room tomorrow, the next day, and the day after that—

"Cody?" Quinn's voice broke Cody's stream of thoughts. The smaller boy looked up to meet Quinn's gaze.

"Won't you change?" Quinn asked, and Cody noticed that the taller boy was now in loose shorts and a cotton shirt.

"Oh, I will," Cody said, looking down at the ground.

Quinn smiled before heading over to Cody. He took hold of the smaller boy's shoulders before leaning in and pecking him square on the forehead.

He stepped away, turning and walking over to the bed. "Come over when you're done okay?" Quinn said, grinning from ear to ear.

Cody nodded, letting out a breath as the sound of his heartbeat in his ears.

Cody took off his shirt, then his shorts before looking through the bag he'd brought with him. He flushed, feeling Quinn's gaze on him.

"You know you can just come up here in your boxers—"

"No," the smaller boy cut him off, as he turned to Quinn with a horrified look on his face.

Quinn chuckled as Cody hurried to throw on a large shirt and some loose shorts. "Ah, I tried."

As Quinn continued to laugh Cody eventually made his way to the bed. He climbed in, snuggling up to Quinn's figure in the dimly lit room. Quinn reached up to flip the light switch just above the bed's headboard so that the room went dark. They stayed silent, the two of them breathing in a synced rhythm.

"I'm glad you're here," Quinn said as he moved his hand under Cody's shirt before pressing a kiss to the boy's forehead.

Cody buried his head in Quinn's shoulder as he shivers under the boy's touch. Although not said out loud it was like a silent 'I love you' floated in the air as the two boys touched and kissed each other in the dark.

"I said no a while back..." Cody trailed when Quinn pulled away from him. "I was just nervous," he muttered, letting himself look into Quinn's dark eyes.

"Do you want to try this night? I've still got all the stuff we bought," Quinn said, raising his body so that he was hovering over Cody a bit.

"Yeah..." Cody trailed remembering the condoms and lube the boys had bought with red faces. "If you want..."

"Alright," Quinn said, rolling out of bed before heading for his dresser again. He was trying to play it cool, but he was also nervous. "We don't have to go all the way today. We can just work on being comfortable. How does that sound?" Quinn asked, walking over to the bed with the condom pack and the small lotion bottle.

Cody nodded, sitting up before crawling behind Quinn. He rested his head on the taller boy's shoulder, looking out into the room as the two of them listened to each other's breathing.

"Is there anything you want us to do exactly...?" Quinn asked, his voice small and almost inaudible. "Like any position, stuff to do, that kind of stuff?" he added when Cody remained silent.

The smaller boy felt his face heat up. "Just tell me if you like it." Cody wanted that a lot. He wanted Quinn to like being with him so much that it was a need.

"Oh," Quinn said, turning to look at Cody. Their noses were so close, almost touching. "That's a given, don't you think?"

Cody stared at him, feeling his face become hot. Yes, Quinn said he liked him all the time, but as much as he was happy that they would go through with this he was also scared. Guys liked curves and full chests. Cody was skinny and slender. He wondered if Quinn would still like him when they were both butt naked.

"Hey," Quinn said, making Cody blink. He hadn't realized when he had spaced out. "Kiss me," the boy said, smiling a bit before leaning in to catch Cody's lips. The smaller boy moaned, always a sucker for the full lips that seemed to overwhelm his smaller ones.

Quinn pulled away, taking off his top, and Cody did the same before watching Quinn take off his pants.

"Come on," Quinn urged, reaching out to pull the band of the boy's trousers. Cody's face heated up, and he nodded, letting Quinn help him out of his shorts. He was naked now, just like Quinn, and his fear that Quinn wouldn't be as interested when he saw him completely naked started to overwhelm him.

"Gosh, you're so lovely." Cody's fears melted away with Quinn's words as the taller boy reached out to usher him to his lap to straddle him. "Look at you..." Quinn said, running a hand through the boy's dark hair before letting both his hands run up and down his back before settling on his waist.

Quinn stared at Cody, letting his thumb fingers kneed the boy's small stomach fat—people who didn't exercise didn't have rock hard stomachs, even if they were skinny, Quinn knew that but his head had never imagined that touching the soft mold would make him so horny—that's why he was so quick to slip his hand under Cody's shirt when they kissed. His mind fogged as he wondered if it would jiggle a bit when they had sex—

Quinn closed his eyes, feeling his stomach twist with want as his lower half hardened just beneath Cody's bum. "I need a moment to think a bit," Quinn said in a breathy voice as he opened his eyes. He let his hand move to the happy trail of dark hair that pointed towards Cody's privates.

He took a deep breath, looking up at Cody again before kissing him. The smaller boy wrapped his hand around Quinn's shoulders as they kissed, grinding on him as Quinn touched his chest and pulled at his nipples.

"Cody wait..." Quinn muttered, holding the boy's hips so that he would stop moving. "I don't want to come yet," he muttered, pulling away from

Cody whose face was flushed red. Cody nodded, staying still as the two boys rested with their foreheads touching as they shared occasional kisses.

At a point, Quinn pulled Cody up and laid him down on the bed. He reached out for the lube and condom pack he'd tossed aside a while back. He took a condom out, slipping a finger into it before applying some lube. He stared down at Cody, feeling a bit nauseous yet flattered that the boy had left his wellbeing up to him.

He really didn't want to hurt him or make him cry. Cody had cried enough in his lifetime.

"Let's see if it works," he muttered, pushing a finger into the boy. It had felt weird at first, but soon Cody's toes were curling from how good it felt. One, two, three fingers after Cody felt like he was on fire. Quinn was stroking his shaft, asking if it made it hurt less. The taller boy crawled up a bit, letting himself suck on Cody in hopes that it would cloud the pain as he attempted the fourth finger.

Cody bucked and frowned for a while, but otherwise, he seemed content.

"Okay, I think it's alright," Quinn muttered, looking down. "Wait a minute," he said, scolding himself for not starting off with a condom. He rushed one on himself, and the two boys laughed, easing the pressure a bit. Quinn returned to hovering over Cody, and he tried his best to go slow.

It took some time. Countless squeaks, complaints and back scratches from Cody later, Quinn had eased in as far as he could.

He didn't start moving until he was sure Cody was ready, and when he did, he took his time. The weird mix of pain and pleasure was starting to subside for just pleasure, and Cody had the strength to open his eyes and look up at Quinn. The boy's eyes were closed, and his face would contort in pleasure when a shiver ran through him.

It was hot, but not hot enough. Cody wanted Quinn to say how he felt. He wanted the boy to tell him that he was the one doing this to him.

In porn, the actors would ask how the top was feeling. Cody wanted Quinn to say stuff, but he was too shy to encourage it.

His mind flooded with pleasure at Quinn's next thrust, and he let out a deep moan, feeling himself quiver as Quinn slowed down and stroked the area.

"I think I found the area," Quinn muttered, leaning into the boy. "Where you feel good," Quinn explained, planting a kiss on Cody's head as he started moving again. Cody understood what he meant—his prostate or however it was pronounced.

The shivers kept coming, and the moans and sighs kept escaping Cody's lips. The boy looked up at Quinn, feeling his face flush red at the sight of ecstasy on the boy's face.

That was because of him. That was because Quinn enjoyed being with him.

Cody felt a bit brave. "Quinn?" he asked in a soft voice, making the dark-haired boy's eyes peel open a bit. "Does it feel good?"

Quinn seemed a bit taken aback, but he licked his lips, nodding his head. "Yeah..."

Cody's heart skipped. "Can you tell me how...?" he asked, in a slightly louder voice, feeling his body flood with confidence.

Quinn seemed a bit shy, but he didn't avoid the question. "You're so warm and tight. I'm a bit scared I'll finish early, and that's why I keep pausing..." he trailed, adjusting them both by pulling Cody closer by the hips as he arched over the boy. "It's nice to look at you get hard too. Also, it's your whole body's flushed red. It's super cute..." Quinn was rambling now, and Cody was quivery as his stomach knotted with happiness.

"The look on your face is so cute. Oh God your lips," Quinn muttered, increasing his pace as he leaned forward to kiss Cody. "They're so cute."

Cody bucked a bit when Quinn moved to suck on his nipple.

"I could suck on you if you pull out fast," Cody muttered and Quinn raised his head.

The taller boy frowned a bit. "But I'll cum in your mouth."

"Yeah, I know," Cody said, feeling his face warm up. Just like he wanted.

Quinn didn't question that, and he picked up his pace, and the two moaned as the bed creaked.

"Your stomach's so cute when it jiggles like this..." Quinn trailed and Cody followed Quinn's eyes to his stomach. It was indeed jiggling a bit, due to Quinn's fast pace. His eyes loved to the sight of Quinn pulling in and out of him. It looked amazing. Cody quivered, letting out a moan as he came on Quinn's chest, and Quinn pulled out, taking off his condom before holding his hand over his head.

Cody crawled over, taking hold of Quinn before stroking him and kissing his tip. He licked it a few times, before making to suck on it. Quinn could feel his legs shaking from the pressure. It didn't help that Cody would press down on him, and then move back to licking between his slit.

The boy groaned, feeling his mind fog up as he reached his peak.

"Cody..." he trailed, managing to pull the boy away, but not far enough for the first stream to hit his face.

"I'm sorry..." he muttered, but Cody surprised him by reaching out to keep stroking him, and he watched as the boy just sat there, letting the streams of cum pour on his face.

What had just happened hadn't dawned on Quinn quite yet, until the post-sex clarity kicked in.

"Jesus," he yelled, getting out of bed before looking for the nearest thing to wipe Cody's face. "I'm so sorry..." he trailed, making Cody giggle as he wiped as his face with a fresh bedsheet he'd pulled out of his drawer.

The two boys cuddled in bed together afterward. They'd figured the sex thing out just fine like Quinn had promised they would, and Cody's fears had not been confirmed. Quinn liked him as he was. Skinny, hairy and slender—a boy. He decided that he would try his best to stop worrying about pretty girls that liked Quinn.

CHAPTER THIRTY

- -

There's an ongoing game on the basketball court. Quinn is playing with his friends, dribbling, throwing, catching and blocking. It was noisy, the boys laughed, yelled and made sharp sounds on the clay floor with their sneakers as they ran around. Cody was sitting on the stairs by the gates, watching Quinn with a smile on his face. It felt like de Ja Vu. It had been two months since he'd started living with Quinn's family. His skin looked richer, his eyes looked brighter, and he'd put on some weight thanks to Quinn's mother's cooking.

Also, keeping up with Quinn meant exercising a lot. The boy walked around a fair amount, and he was prone to breaking out into runs, leaving Cody and to run after him.

"Be careful! If the ball hits Cody, Quinn will have our heads!" Hozier yelled when the basketball bounced off the metal netting that surrounded the court.

The other boys chuckled at that as the game paused for a moment. Quinn had come out to his friends slowly—one by one, and to everyone at once when he had forgotten it was supposed to be private. He had jumped Cody, pressing a kiss to the boy's lips in front of everyone, and had only pulled away when Karl had coughed. It had been a little difficult to explain, but his friends didn't seem too fazed. Some of them even mentioned guessing the situation months ago.

Hozier walked over to where the ball had rolled before throwing it back into the court and starting the game again. Cody smiled when he spotted Quinn looking his way. The taller boy was in shorts that rode a bit up his toned thighs, and the tank top he was wearing was drenched in sweat. Quinn smiled back at Cody, waving before he got yelled at by Karl to pay attention.

Cody watched them continue the game, and when they were done and left the basketball court, Quinn walked up to him. The taller boy's forehead was dripping with sweat, and his wavy hair was a mess that stuck to his forehead and neck. Most people wouldn't have let Quinn touch them with a ten-foot pole in his state, but Cody just laughed, hugging him briefly before taking his hand.

The two started to walk home together, leaving before the others. The afternoon was long today—it was six, but the sun was persistent with its rays of yellow light. Summer days were like that with its long days and short nights.

The sound of their feet crunching the sand with the bottom of their shoes was the only sound for miles. Quinn squeezed Cody's hand, looking over the boy as he thought of what to say. "Are you following Janet to work tomorrow?" he asked.

"Yes," Cody said with a smile as he looked at Quinn from the side of his eyes. He noticed that the boy was frowning a bit, making Cody's eyes go wide with concern.

"What's wrong?" Cody asked, moving closer to Quinn so that their sides were brushing as they walled.

"Nah, ignore me," Quinn sighed, forcing himself to smile. "I just liked you coming over to the mechanic's shop, that's all." The taller boy brushed back his hair with his free hand as Cody giggled, rolling his eyes. Quinn liked him being close, and that was one of the reasons Cody followed him to the basketball court even though he never joined to play.

Quinn had started working as an apprentice at a mechanics shop, and Janet had recommended Cody to her boss when she had figured out the boy was a fast learner. They had bonded when Janet had cut Cody's mess of a hair, and Cody had offered to do hers in return. Cody would start at the salon tomorrow. Cody spent most of his time messing with Janet, and Quinn's mother's hair, so there wouldn't be a difference if he helped in the hairdressing salon Janet worked at and got paid for it.

"Should we get drinks? We should get drinks," Quinn said when the two got closer to the local convenience store. He tugged Cody's had, making the boy laugh as he followed him along.

There was a nostalgia that came with walking into the run-down shack with Quinn. They had their proper first conversation on its staircase, they had bought their first pack of condoms here together, and they had kissed on the stairs at the back for the first time. Cody remembered feeling that Quinn wasn't so scary for the first time when Quinn offered to buy him snacks.

They both walked up the stair and went in, and after a while, they both came out with bottles of soft drinks. They didn't linger behind like they used to and continued to head home.

Quinn took out the bottle cap with his teeth before spitting it out in the distance. "After we've saved up enough, we can get a small place together. What do you think?" he asked, taking a swing of his soft drink.

Cody smiled. "I'd like that." He liked living with Quinn's family, but it also meant being quiet when they did things together or planning intimate moments around his parents and sister's schedule. He liked the idea of just being with Quinn a lot. To be quite honest, anywhere with Quinn was home to Cody.

Quinn mirrored the smile. "Great, I want to be the one taking care of you for a change. Mum does that a lot, but I'm the one dating you."

Cody laughed as he rolled his eyes at his boyfriend. "Don't be ridiculous. Are you jealous of your mum?"

Quinn pouted. "Yes, sort of?" His words made Cody's face warm up.

Gosh, he's too honest! Cody thought, trying to stop his heart from breaking out of his ribcage.

"Alright, I'll start calling you by your mum's name, so you won't get jealous anymore, how's that?" Cody asked, playing off his flustered self with a joke. Quinn laughed, and so did Cody. The walk became silent again until Cody spoke up.

"I want to take care of you too," Cody said under his breath, squeezing Quinn's hand. The taller boy heard him, and a grin got plastered on his face.

The two boys continued their way home, talking as their faces mirrored expressions of love, happiness, and gratitude. This was the happiest Cody had ever been. Sharing himself with someone was something he hadn't thought would be possible in a million years, and he was glad Quinn had reached out to him when he'd seemed invisible behind the gates.

THE END